CODE
BEGGARMAN

PAT MONTEATH

A Quill Publishing Book

Published by Quill Publishing in 2007

ISBN 978-0-9545914-4-1

06102007-1

First published in 2007 in the United Kingdom by
Quill Publishing
The Haven Eskdaleside,
Grosmont,
Whitby, North Yorkshire YO22 5PS.

Although based on real events, characters, names, dates, times, companies, organisations, and agencies in this novel have been changed and are either the product of the author's imagination or, if real, used fictitiously without any intent to describe their actual conduct.

Acknowledgements

This would not have been possible without the unwavering support of Anne and my family who have had to put up with my many late nights and lack of time spent with them whilst writing this book. Nor would it have been possible without the Apprentice or the main characters that shall remain nameless to protect their anonymity, but they know who they are.

Remember your friends, but whatever you do, do not forget your enemies!

Pat Montealt

Preface

Having been one of the top operators within the Department, Richard James suffered the ignominy of being retired early, the reason given by his superiors was that he had suffered a breakdown and for his own protection was sectioned. However, Richard knew otherwise, and on leaving Chartham - a large psychiatric hospital in Kent - he vowed that with Paul's help he would prove his innocence and show the powers that be that he was betrayed and used as a scapegoat.

Sir James Johnstone – a top Civil Servant in charge of a branch within the Secret Intelligence Service – is contacted by Mr Gilpin, the man from the Ministry. Mr Gilpin has been charged with the task of eliciting help from the SIS to seek out a mole and a traitor. Apparently the Department has lost a number of good operators over the years and many recent operations have failed. Gilpin suggests that perhaps Sir James may know someone, someone who is either retired from the Service or an ex Military Intelligence Officer who would undertake such a task *'unofficially of course, as the Government could not be seen to be connected with the investigation.'* Sir James agrees to consider the proposal and promises to get back to him in due course.

Richard's chance to clear his name and so regain control of his life comes much sooner than he anticipated, and with his good friend Paul Jones he sets about retracing his tracks which leads him back to Ireland and the beautiful Fionnuala who has a confession to make. Upon his return to Ireland he meets up with Jean O'Donald who has become a close friend since the death of her husband. Sean O'Donald, Jean's late husband, had been Richard's friend and handler through the 1970s and 1980s until a car bomb resulted in his untimely death. Whilst in Ireland Richard enlists the help of a number of old friends and acquaintances and with their help he launches the operation

ii

codenamed Beggarman, an operation to track down the mole codenamed *Thief* and prove his innocence. The net is cast far and wide and spreads throughout Ireland and across the Irish Sea to London and the Home Counties. Who is the traitor, who is the mole, who is the *Thief!*

As in the previous two titles the reader is taken into the twilight zone of subterfuge, covert operations, undercover agents and the secret world of 'spooks' and double agents. Richard and Paul between them, piece together an interesting picture that has resounding repercussions in high places and results in the final chapter of the Ferryman trilogy.

Chapter 1

England was sweltering in a late summer heatwave and with temperatures up in the eighties many of the local workforce were spending their lunch break out in the park either sunbathing, or taking a leisurely stroll. The Serpentine looked cool and inviting as the noon day sun glinted on its surface and a small group of ducks slowly cruised around in the distance. The city gent, with bowler hat and pin-striped suit, looked a little overdressed for such a hot day as he, deep in conversation with another man, paused at the water's edge to feed the ducks. His companion, a tall distinguished gentleman with steel grey hair, looked a little less incongruous on such a hot day as he was dressed in an open necked short sleeved shirt and light grey trousers.

"Well Sir James, thank you for coming at such short notice," the city gent addressed his companion, "I do of course realise that this must be terribly inconvenient for you and I really appreciate you giving up your valuable time to talk to me." He paused, gave a little cough as if to clear his throat before continuing. "It's a rather ticklish situation I find myself in and I don't quite know where to begin. Of course the Government cannot be seen to be taking any active part in this and that is why I thought that someone of your standing may be able to help us in this matter." He threw the last piece of bread to the greedy ducks, emptied the bag of any crumbs then carefully folded it before placing it in his pocket. "Shall we walk Sir James?"

"If you wish to Mr Gilpin."

"Then after you Sir James."

Sir James nodded his acknowledgement and set off at a leisurely pace taking the path that circumnavigated the Serpentine in a clockwise direction. As they strolled gently along the bank of the Serpentine Gilpin looking flushed with the heat, removed his bowler hat and taking out a freshly ironed handkerchief proceeded to wipe the beads of sweat from his forehead.

"Phew, this temperature, I'm pleased we have air conditioning in the office otherwise it would certainly be unbearable. I assume your office is air conditioned Sir James?" He wiped the handkerchief around the headband inside the hat and then carefully repositioned it back on his head.

"Oh yes it certainly is Mr Gilpin, but I sense we are not here to discuss the ramifications of air conditioning, or to take an afternoon stroll in the park are we Mr Gilpin?" If Gilpin took exception to the mild admonishment he certainly didn't show it.

"Well the situation is Sir James that the PM is somewhat concerned about the escalation of losses that seem to be occurring in Ulster. The enemy seems to be constantly one jump ahead; it is as if they know our plans way before we do." He paused and cast a glance toward Sir James to reassure himself that what he had just said about the concern of the Prime Minister had not gone unnoticed, and then he continued. "There have been suggestions that there may be a mole operating within our Intelligence Service, but Ashford and Lisburn have both drawn a blank. Now you've met the Colonel at Ashford; huh, his name escapes me for the present…"

"Ash," interjected Sir James, "Colonel Ash."

"Ah yes that's the man Ash. Now Ash is adamant that his right hand man O'Rourke has had some of his best operatives working round the clock on this one and up until now they have been unable to find the leak." Again Gilpin looked toward Sir James for some reaction.

"Well Gilpin go on."

"Of course Sir James. Now where was I?"

"You were saying O'Rourke couldn't find…"

"Ah yes of course," he interrupted Sir James. "As I was saying, he couldn't find the leak and now O'Rourke is suggesting that the leak may be within the RUC. In fact he has suggested that information is being leaked from Special Branch, but of course Home Office is strongly denying such a thing and who could blame them? But O'Rourke is adamant that it is in their back yard so to speak. Of course, I've already spoken to Brigadier Townsend, incidentally have you ever met him?"

"Yes on one occasion, seemed a very capable man to me."

"Yes nice fellow. Anyway Townsend, he's now overall in charge of Military Intelligence in Ulster and Ash answers to him, has now gone to his Chief of Staff stating that the leak must be either MI5 or Special Branch. He is strongly denying that the problem is at Ashford or Lisburn and the whole thing has now become a major embarrassment for the Government. What's more I'm told that Britain is now the laughing stock of the IRA." He glanced again at Sir James. "It does rather seem that the enemy have managed to penetrate our Intelligence network or else they are better at the game than we are! Neither way is acceptable Sir James and the problem now is if, and it is a big if, we have a leak then we need to find it urgently."

"So Mr Gilpin, why come to me?"

"Well, it's like this Sir James; whoever we use to trace this leak must not be traced back to the Government." Sir James raised one eyebrow questioning what Gilpin had just said.

"And why is that Mr Gilpin?"

"With respect Sir James, I would have thought that was obvious."

"No, not at all so please elucidate."

"Well Sir James, should anything go wrong..."

"Is it likely to?" Sir James interrupted Gilpin.

"Err no, but if it should..." Gilpin left the sentence unfinished.

Gilpin you are squirming. So to cover your backside and to make life easy you want to enlist my help to pull the red hot chestnuts out of the fire.

"So, let me get this straight Mr Gilpin, you have been asked, no instructed by Downing Street, to speak to me about a potential leak or mole within the Intelligence Service, why?"

"As I said Sir James, the PM is gravely concerned and has decided to handle this matter personally with strict instructions that whoever undertakes the task to trap this… err…mole should not be seen to be employed by Her Majesty's Government."

"But you haven't told me why my department should be involved; after all we have enough of our own problems, what with budgetary controls being talked about, cut-backs in expenditure and less funding being made available so why should the department take on other's work for which they are being duly paid to do?"

"Ah, a good point Sir James. All I can say is that your department may have the right kind of approach. In fact it is quite conceivable that you may personally know of someone who may consider undertaking such a task; of course should anything go wrong…" Once again Gilpin left the sentence unfinished.

"So are you suggesting that it's all right for me to be embarrassed as long as the PM's department is in the clear?"

"No, not at all. All I am saying is that perhaps you know of someone who could undertake such a project and is very, very discreet about it. After all neither of us wants to be embarrassed. Therefore whoever you or should I say we use cannot be seen to be employed by the Government. The fact of the matter is the Government cannot be seen to be linked with an investigation that is carried out through the back door."

I bet they can't and yet they expect me to carry out an investigation without so much as by your leave. I should coco!

"Supposing there is someone, then how do they get recompensed?" Gilpin didn't answer.

Huh, I bet you never considered that and I'm damned if I am financing it out of my budget.

They walked on in silence for a short distance.

"I had hoped you would see it as part of your brief Sir James and subsequently part of your funding."

"What! You are of course joking…"

"Hmm. In that case I suppose we could of course make a sum available…"

"I should hope you could Mr Gilpin," was the curt response from Sir James. "After all if we are to supply the manpower and run the risks to boot, then the very least the Government could do is to fund it."

"If we were to fund such a project Sir James, then it would be in the nature of a one-off payment into a non-traceable offshore bank account. Would you find that an acceptable compromise?"

"That sounds fine in principle, but it may pose certain problems. How about the Government making an extraordinary non-recurring payment into the department's overseas account, now if that could be done then that would be better?"

"It is possible."

"In that case I will give the project my undivided attention."

"Thank you Sir James, after all there may be someone suitable who wouldn't be linked back to the Government. May be someone who has had experience of this sort of work and has retired, or there may be someone who is ex-forces who could be trusted. I'll wait to hear from you." Sir James and Mr Gilpin shook hands and went their separate ways.

Later that afternoon Sir James went downstairs to the basement where they stored the archived files. He spoke briefly to the young lady in the Office and a few moments later she stepped out of the lift on the eighth floor and walked the short distance to Christine Delahey's office. Christine Delahey had been PA to Sir James Johnstone, the head of the 'circus', for a number of years and had enjoyed every last minute of the job. There was a light tap on her door.

"Come in." The door opened and a young twenty year old bounced into her room.

"Hi, I've been sent up to get some papers for Sir James." Christine Delahey looked questioningly at the twenty year old.

"Sir James sent you up you said?"

"Yes, for these papers or documents or something." She handed Christine the note that Sir James had scribbled out.

Strange, why send her up here with a note when he could have phoned up for them. Ah well not to worry.

She opened the folded sheet and looked at what he had scribbled shrugged her shoulders and opened one of the grey filing cabinets and started to thumb her way through the drawer packed full of buff manila files.

"Are you sure this is the correct file name?" she asked the twenty year old.

"Yeah, as far as I know." She shrugged her shoulders, "he didn't say much, just came in the office and asked for some paper and scribbled down what you have there, why do you ask?"

"Oh…no reason, just that they are not where he said they were. I wondered if he had got the project number wrong that's all. I'm sorry, but this could take me a little while to sort out so why don't you go and grab yourself a coffee from the canteen along the corridor." She flashed a smile at the young lady.

"Are you sure that'll be all right, I mean up here on the executive floor and all that, will they let me in?" Christine gave a little chuckle.

"Of course it's all right, and yes, they will let you in. We're no different up here you know. Go on go get yourself a coffee. Tell them I sent you and to book it to Sir James."

"Well if you're sure and thank you…err…may I call you Christine?"

"Of course you can. Now go. I'll come and find you when I've found the files." The twenty year old didn't need a second invitation; she was out through the door and heading off down the corridor to the executive's coffee lounge.

Now where on earth are these files?

Christine made her way through to the inner sanctum, as she called it, the office belonging to her boss and head of the 'circus' Sir James Johnstone. The first place she looked was on his desk but to no avail, then she moved to his cupboard and continued to hunt for the elusive documentation.

Sir James looked up in the archived records the reference number for a file headed *Operation Orpheus*. Armed with the number written on a piece of scrap paper Sir James walked unhurriedly along the never-ending rows of metal shelving. Each row held box files from floor to ceiling, each one having its own special reference number. He looked at the piece of paper in his hand that he had written the number on.

It must be around here somewhere. Ah there it is.

Reaching up he lifted down a dusty box file and carefully he blew off the excess dust from the top and opened it. Inside was a manila folder on the front of which was stamped TOP SECRET and the project name *Operation Orpheus*. Sir James removed the folder and thumbed through the pages to make sure it was all intact. Having satisfied himself everything he needed was there he carefully replaced the box file back on the shelf and returned to the Archive Office. Picking up the phone he dialled his office number and waited. He didn't have to wait too long before a female's voice answered.

"Christine Delahey speaking."

"Ah, Christine. Any luck with those papers?"

"Sorry Sir James, I haven't come across them yet. I'm blowed if I know where to look next."

"Well leave it then. I'll sort it out later; I think I know where I can lay my hands on them," he said knowing full well he had them all the time. He had concealed the documents inside his newspaper that he had carried with him from his office down to the basement. He had done this on purpose in order to get some time alone in the Archive section whilst the young clerk was waiting for Christine to find the non-existent papers. Now all he needed to do was to photocopy some of the information held in the manila file that he had taken out of the box file, and that would only take a couple of minutes. He would be through in no time at all, photocopies done, papers back in the manila folder, the folder replaced in the box file and the box file back on the rack where it came from. All would be as it was by the time the young clerk returned and he would be back in his office.

Half an hour later Sir James was back in his office reading up on the background of a field operative whose codename was Ferryman.

This man had been good, bloody good.

This was quite true until something had gone wrong. Sir James continued to read through the information before him and was surprised to read that Ferryman had taken early retirement.

Strange, why did he take early retirement, usually if someone takes early retirement their record gives the reason but there's no reason given?

To say he was a little puzzled by the omission was an understatement so he carefully re-read the information searching for clues, any clues that would indicate what had really happened. It was whilst he was reading through the document for the second time he noticed a comment written in the margin. With the handwriting being so small and faded it was no wonder that he had missed it initially, but now with eyes straining he could just about make out an odd word or two. The names Dr Ferris, Woolwich and Richard James were just about discernible along with the word scapegoat.

How did this Dr Ferris fit in with Richard James and where was he from? Could it be that he was a scapegoat or was the note referring to Richard James being made a scapegoat? Was the person named Dr Ferris a medical practitioner or not and the name Woolwich, did this refer to the Arsenal or to the military hospital at Woolwich?

Sir James leaned back in his chair and stared up at the ceiling.

If only I could get some answers to these questions then that would shed some light on why such a good operator had retired early.

"I wonder," he said out loud. He picked up his phone and dialled a number and waited. There was a click as the phone at the other end was lifted and a man with an Irish accent answered.

"Irish Desk."

"James here. Come up to my office please."

"Certainly Sir James."

A minute or two later his white phone buzzed and the light against Christine's name flashed.

"Yes Christine."

"Jimmy from the Irish Desk is here to see you Sir James."

"Good send him in." There was a gentle tap on his door. "Come in," he called as he casually placed a copy of The Times newspaper over the documents he'd just been reading.

"You wanted to see me Sir James."

"Yes Jimmy come in and grab one of those chairs over by the table and bring it over here." Sir James said indicating the two chairs placed either side of a small occasional table on the far side of his office. "You were in Lisburn back in the eighties weren't you Jimmy?"

"Yes Sir."

"Did you ever meet a guy called James, Richard James?"

"Richard James" Jimmy repeated the name "Yes of course Sir James, I remember Richard. I was his controller for a while."

"So what do you know about Mr James?"

"Nice bloke Sir, but he was retired early through ill health."

"Oh, that's strange…"

"What's strange Sir James?"

"That you say he retired early through ill health."

"Well he did, and there was nobody more surprised than me when we were told about it."

"Oh I'm sure that what you say is totally true, but there is no mention of his early retirement through ill health anywhere in his file."

"Are you sure Sir James?"

"Oh I'm sure all right."

"Is it possible that you may have overlooked it, or a page of his file has been misplaced?"

"I suppose I could have overlooked it and it's always a possibility that a page may have been misplaced, but I don't think so."

"That's odd. I know that minor things sometimes go unrecorded, but Richard was a top class operator and I would certainly have expected some mention of it in his records."

"Well, I've been through his file a number of times and as far as I can make out there is no mention of his being ill, unless of course it's as you say, a document or page is missing."

So the plot thickens!

"What was wrong with him?" Sir James asked.

"Some sort of breakdown I believe, but you say it's not recorded on his file Sir James?"

Something like that should have been recorded.

"Not that I recollect though I could be mistaken. A breakdown you say?"

There's something not quite right about this.

"Yes Sir James, well that's what we were told."

"Tell me about this Richard James."

"What do you want to know Sir James?"

"Well was he reliable, was he a good field man, that type of thing?"

"Well, he was one of the best, reliable and a stickler for detail, very thorough in everything he did. In the main he was a safe operator..."

"How do you mean 'a safe operator'?" enquired Sir James.

"He didn't take chances, he minimised the risks and maximised the gains. Whenever he took a risk he would always cater for it and any fall out from it. His risks were always calculated risks never a gamble. He played by the rules and where his team members were concerned safety was paramount. Then it happened..."

"What happened?" asked Sir James

"Well suddenly out of the blue the department was told that Richard had been invalided out, declared medically unfit. In fact when I was told that he'd had a breakdown, you could have knocked me over with a feather."

"Why?"

"Because in my mind he was the last person ever to have a breakdown, he was an ex-Para and had gone through the SAS training. Basically, he was just so mentally together and physically fit I didn't believe it, I couldn't believe it. In fact when Sean O'Donald, a mate of his in the UDR bought it, he spent a lot of time over in Lisburn looking after Jean, Sean's wife. Also, he was the one who got Austen out. On top of all that he then had the raid on 'slab' Riley's place dumped at his feet, and that went pear shaped big time. What with one of the team getting killed and one badly shot, he was lucky to get out of that unscathed. Then to cap it all, after they'd got clear, both he and Wyman became the target of the Provos whilst holed up in a so called safe house. The safe house was attacked and their car was blown up outside. All of this happened over a twenty-four hour period and boy was he angry."

"Angry hmm. Would you say he was pushed to his limit?"

"No way Sir James. Sure he was angry all right, he felt let down by us, but he was certainly not teetering on the edge and that's why I was surprised when they said he'd had a breakdown." Sir James mulled over what Jimmy had just said.

So, here is a man the pinnacle of fitness, mentally alert and a hardened operator who suddenly decides to up and leave the Service and yet according to 'Official' sources he had had a breakdown, now if that was the case then why wasn't it logged as such? It doesn't make sense, unless somebody had been careless and left the faintly scribbled note on the file in error, in which case the word 'scapegoat' referred to Richard James.

"That's very interesting, very interesting indeed. What do you reckon Jimmy? Do you think he was setup?" Jimmy looked puzzled.

Do you know something about this that we don't Sir James? He took his time and thought carefully about his answer and decided that there was nothing to gain by lying.

"Yes, I'm convinced he was. I'm convinced someone somewhere high up wanted him out of the way." Sir James leaned back in his chair and stared thoughtfully at Jimmy through his half closed eyes.

"Why do you think that Jimmy?"

"May be he knew too much Sir." Sir James, remembering what he had seen scribbled in the margin of the file, took a moment or two to ponder.

"You know you may well have a point there Jimmy and what is more you could well be closer to the truth than you think. Thank you Jimmy that will be all."

"Thank you Sir James." Jimmy stood up and put the chair back where it belonged and was already on his way out when Sir James stopped him in his tracks with a strange request.

"Jimmy, I would prefer you not to mention anything about this meeting to anyone outside of this office. In fact I will go one stage further and say that this meeting never ever happened. I'm sure you understand." Sir James tapped his temple, smiled and gave a knowing wink.

"Of course Sir James," Jimmy smiled briefly. "What meeting?" he asked as he turned to go out the door. Sir James waited a few minutes, just long enough to allow Jimmy to get out of earshot before he picked up his telephone and called Mr Gilpin at the Ministry.

"Ah Gilpin, Sir James here. About our earlier discussion, I think I may have got a possible candidate."

Chapter 2

Sunday lunchtime was always a good time to be in the Woodman's Hall, especially about one o'clock because it was at this time that whelks and roast potatoes appeared on the bar for those who wanted them. The atmosphere was convivial and the beer flowed.

"Come on Richard drink up. Mine's a pint and it's your turn to buy."

"Yeah, come on you're holding up proceedings." Richard wasn't really listening to his mates because someone had just walked over his grave. He put down his glass and made his way into the other bar, glancing over towards the dartboard on his way to the toilet.

He was sure he had recognised the voice but he couldn't see anyone in the bar that he didn't know. There it was again, this time he was certain he had heard the voice before, it had come from behind the partition over by the door but the annoying thing was he couldn't see the owner of the voice without walking over to where he thought it came from and that would be too obvious. Damn, why don't you move away from that damn screen so I can see you?

He was certain it belonged to a guy called Wyman who he'd met some years ago in Ashford and had later worked with in Ireland. Unfortunately since then Richard had suffered the ignominy of being sectioned by the Government and spent some time in Chartham Psychiatric Hospital. It had all happened because he had fallen foul of someone high up in the Department. Someone had wanted him out of the way for some reason and had gone to extraordinary lengths to have him labelled as 'mentally unstable'. Because of this he had lost all credibility, his assets had been frozen, he had no credit rating and his passport had been cancelled. In fact that was a period in his life that had cost him dearly; not only in financial terms but also in quality of life and whichever way he had turned he had been unable to get to the bottom of it. Previously he had enjoyed a good contracting business and had been one of the Department's top operators, but that had all gone now, even his army pension had gone! In fact according to records that period of his life, as the Ferryman, had never ever existed. Yes Her Majesty's Government had done a good job all right by having him sectioned. Still that's all in the past, or is it?

"You're back then!" one of Richard's mates stated in a matter of fact way and grinned as Richard reappeared through the door.

"Of course I am. Why, did you think I'd done a runner then?"

"Well it did cross my mind," Terry said jokingly.

"Especially as it's your round," Paul winked at Mick, "so why spoil the habit of a lifetime?" Paul continued to everybody's amusement. Suddenly Paul noticed Richard's face and realised that something was wrong. "Hey, are you OK you look as if you've seen a ghost?"

"I'm fine." Richard replied and made a half-hearted attempt at a smile. Paul was far from convinced.

"Are you sure?" he asked still unconvinced and a frown furrowed his brow. Richard once more smiled and gave a quick shrug of his shoulders and asked in as cheerier voice as he could muster, "Right lads what'll it be?"

This little act didn't fool Paul, he had known Richard for more years than he cared to remember and he knew when something was or was not bugging him. He knew that the smile was a front, it may fool the others but it didn't fool him. His thoughts were interrupted by Richard talking to him.

"Paul do you want another lager or something else this time?"

"Nah, a pint of Stella's fine thanks," he answered absent-mindedly; his thoughts were back on Richard's change in demeanour. He was more interested in what had happened in the interval between Richard leaving the bar and his return. What or who had he seen that had visibly shaken him so?

"Barry, when you're ready." Richard called to the landlord who was in the other bar.

"So what's worried you?" Paul asked in a quiet voice.

"I've all ready told you, nothing."

"You must be joking! I know you well enough by now and I know that between leaving us here and returning something has upset you because when you returned you looked as if you had seen a ghost." Paul muttered through tight lips in Richard's ear, but before he could get a reply Barry, the landlord appeared in the small bar.

"Yes Richard, what can I get you?"

Just in the nick of time thought Richard, *saved by the bell, thanks Barry your timing was impeccable.* "Two pints of bitter and two pints of Stella please."

But Paul was not going to be put off by this little intrusion and continued to push the issue. "So come on Richard out with it." Paul muttered quietly, "who've you seen?"

"No-one. Just leave it, no-one." Richard hissed at Paul, his manner somewhat agitated with this continual probing.

"That'll be seven pounds sixty please."

Richard handed him a ten pound note. "Give Paul the change." he called back over his shoulder as once again he disappeared through to the other bar, just in time to hear the voice he'd heard earlier bidding someone goodbye and to catch a fleeting glimpse of the owner, followed by a bloke with shoulder length hair as they both disappeared through the main door and out into the car park. He was now more than ever convinced that he knew the voice even though he had not seen the person's face, if only he could remember. As for the other person, the one with the long hair, he was certain that his name was Lamar.

Lamar was a man of mystery. He was a person who had appeared on the scene whilst Richard was training a group of men for an operation in Ireland. Unfortunately Operation Orpheus, as the operation had been called, was aborted and it wasn't long after this happened that things started to go pear-shaped for Richard James. He went over to the window in the hope of getting a better look at the two men, but all he could see was a car pull out and drive off up the hill with them in it. He still pondered on the sound of the voice and wondered to whom he was bidding farewell as he returned back to the small lounge bar and his friends.

Richard had forgotten all about the recent incident of the two men and the voice, well that was until Sandy, the landlady, came through to the lounge bar and spotted him chatting with Paul Jones and the rest of the crowd.

"Ah Richard, someone was asking about you in the other bar. If I had realised you were in here I would have sent him through to you."

"Who was it Sandy?" he enquired, recalling his memory of the voice that he had heard and wondering if by chance it was him, all the time hoping she would know but to no avail.

"Sorry Richard, he didn't say his name, but he was very interested in you. I told him you come in here from time to time but that I hadn't seen you today. Sorry about that." Sandy's comment, *'he was very interested in you'* had more than intrigued Richard.

"In what way was he very interested in me?" Richard asked hoping Sandy would be able to throw some light on the mystery person.

"Didn't say anything specific, just sort of asking about you. Wondered if you still lived around here, he said he'd known you for a while but it was a long time ago since he last saw you."

"Did he say when or where he last saw me?"

"No I don't think so. He was just chatting to me in a general sort of way. He didn't stay long, just had the one drink then left, oh he did say he'd pop in again some time." Richard frowned, what was this person's great interest in him.

"What did he look like and was he with anybody?" Richard asked almost in desperation.

"Oh Richard, I don't know." Sandy answered with a slight edge to her voice.

For goodness sake get a life Richard, he was only asking after you.

"Actually Richard, I didn't take much notice of him; I was more interested in beating Peter at darts than talking to him." She gave a false smile to cover up her annoyance at being given the third degree.

After all it wasn't that important so why make such a big thing out of it.

"Not to worry Sandy, no doubt he'll be back if he's desperate to find me." Richard smiled briefly, but all the time he was thinking, *God Sandy; if only you had been a bit more observant...still what's done is done.* He then fell silent. There was a lull in the general conversation; Sandy frowned as she remembered what she had said to him and how he had reacted.

"Actually come to think about it he was a strange bloke, I distinctly remember my words now. What I said was that I hadn't seen you today, but that was not to say you weren't in. I told him to have a quick look through here because you always used the lounge. That's when he said *he couldn't stop* or something *and he would pop back another time.* With that he drank his beer and left with his mate."

"With a mate did you say?"

"Yes." Sandy then turned her attention to Mick. "Sorry Mick are you waiting to be served?" But before Mick could answer Richard asked her about the stranger's friend, and tried to fit the sound of the voice he had heard to the various people he had known or met over the years. He cast his mind back focussing on the images of people such as Breandán O'Shea, Colonel Ash, Major O'Rourke, but none of them fitted the voice. He thought back over the years and the various contacts he had made – some of whom were pretty unsavoury characters at that – he felt that if only Sandy realised and had half a clue then she would probably understand his frustration. Suddenly his thoughts were interrupted by Paul.

"Come on mate you're lagging behind again."

"Sorry, did you say something?" Richard asked absent-mindedly as he was jerked back to the present.

"I said you need to get a move on, you've still got a pint in and it's my shout." But Richard's mind was elsewhere and the Sunday lunchtime session had now lost some of its charm.

"That's OK; leave me out of this round."

"What! Are you off colour or something?" Paul joked. "Hey lads did you hear that, Richard's turned down a pint!" Both Mick and Terry looked at Richard James in mock amazement and Mick continued with the light hearted banter by suggesting that perhaps Richard was sickening for something. Immediately Terry took up the cue and placed the palm of his hand to Richard's brow and pulled it away sharply feigning that it was really hot.

"Phew, he's definitely coming down with something," said Terry shaking his hand as if to cool it down. Then it was Mick's turn to take the mickey.

"Are you sure you're all right Richard, after all turning down a pint…well we don't want you coming over all queer do we lads?" he said with exaggerated concern to which there were guffaws of laughter, but Richard wasn't laughing, in fact he was far from laughing. Suddenly the laughter and merriment evaporated away when Paul noticed his concerned look.

"Hey Richard come on lighten up a little. What's bothering you? You're not still thinking about that old boy in the other bar are you?"

"Actually I am," he answered quite tersely, "but then again it's me that can't remember, and it was me that got put away and lost part of my life so I suppose that's all right." With that he slammed down his empty glass and walked out of the lounge and through to the toilets, only to be followed a few minutes later by Paul.

"Well, what was that all about?" he asked.

"What do you mean?" asked Richard feigning innocence.

"You know what I mean. We were only having a bit of a joke and you go off something alarming. What's rattled your cage?" he asked, annoyed at Richard's little outburst in the lounge. Then it dawned on him. "I know it's that geezer isn't it?" He'd hit the nail right on the head and he knew he had. "Come on own up to it Richard, I'm right aren't I?"

"Yeah you're right; it's that geezer all right." Richard brusquely replied.

"Why, what's he got on you?" Paul asked.

"Paul, if I knew that then I wouldn't be concerned. All I know is that I recognised his voice but I don't know where from. You know, when I was in that place..."

"Do you mean Chartham?"

"No the other place. I lost a part of my life, now all that's there is a blank. Deep down I know that voice but I just can't put a face to it. I've racked my brains and now I'm asking myself was he from that place? Was he something to do with that place? Is he part of that blank? Because in the depths of my mind there is a face but it's totally distorted. It's like trying to see through a thick fog. You know as well as I do that the Government stitched me up and in my heart I know that voice is from around that time. So why is he here and what is he doing asking questions about me?" Richard fell silent.

"I don't know is the honest answer, but if it worries you that much then you need to do what you've always said you would do…"

"And what's that Paul?"

"Start to dig. Start by working your way backwards and try to find out exactly what happened and why. I've already told you I will help in whatever way I can, so do it Richard do it."

"OK, so where do I start?"

"Hmm…good point, at this moment I'm not sure but let's both think it through and get together during the week and work out some sort of plan." He thought about Paul's suggestion for a moment or two and then he slowly nodded his head. He seemed a little unsure at first, but the more he thought about it the more he warmed to it.

"OK, yes OK," he said, "I think we'll need to go back to Ireland." Once he had accepted the situation in his mind the easier it got and he started to gabble quickly. "Yes the more I think about Ireland the more I believe that's where some of the answers are. Let's do it, let's start putting the pieces of jigsaw together. What do you reckon; do you think we should start in Ireland?" He was now excited at the prospect, so much so that Paul for once became the stabilising influence, the brake, the one to hold things in check, whereas in the past this role had always been Richard's.

"Slow down, slow down. Not so fast, let's just look at what we have first before we get ahead of ourselves. Leave it at that for now."

"OK then I'll give you a call during the week and we'll get together then." Richard's eyes said it all. For the first time in a long time they held that glow of life, the old cunning was returning to the old master. At last he could see a purpose to life. At last he felt ready for the challenges that lay ahead of him and he now felt a lot happier because at last he had made the decision to try to clear his name.

On Wednesday evening, just as Richard picked up the phone to ring Paul, the flap of his letter box rattled and a white envelope gently fluttered to the floor. He was not aware of any footsteps, nor did anyone knock on the door. Intrigued to know who was hand delivering notes through his letter box at 8:00 pm on a Wednesday night he hurriedly replaced the phone and wrenched open the front door. He wasn't quick enough. All he managed to do was to catch a fleeting glimpse of a shadowy figure as he or she disappeared into the darkness.

Leaving the front door wide open Richard rushed out into the night.

"Oi, hang on a minute," he called after them, but to no avail. Helped by the background light that spilled from the front door illuminating his front path, Richard ran as fast as he could to the front gate, but again was just too late. From just inside the gate he caught a glimpse of the person as they opened their car door but only for a second before they had slammed it shut followed by a low powerful growl from the car's engine as it accelerated away. By the time he had reached the pavement, the red glow from the car's tail lights was no more than two small discs of red in the distance. It was obvious that they, whoever they were, either didn't hear Richard call to them or ignored him. He felt that the latter was the most likely.

"Damn it." he muttered under his breath as he turned and walked back down the path. Back indoors he at once retrieved the envelope that had come to rest on the front door mat. It was addressed to Richard James in the finest copperplate handwriting he had ever seen. Richard turned the envelope over and over again, examining it for some giveaway clue, but apart from his name, in handwriting he didn't recognise, there was little else of any significance to be seen. Opening the envelope revealed a single sheet of good quality notepaper which had been neatly and carefully folded exactly in half fitting snugly into the envelope. Richard withdrew the single sheet of paper and unfolded it to reveal the name Sir James Johnstone heavily embossed upon it, but no address. The letter was cryptic in its content and read: -

Sir James Johnstone

Dear Mr James,
I have something that I feel will be of great interest to you so I look forward to meeting with you tomorrow night. I have booked a table in your name at the County Hotel, Canterbury. Meet me for dinner 7:30 sharp to discuss this.

Regards,

Sir James Johnstone
PS. On no account must you convey the contents of this note to anyone. This meeting is highly confidential and must remain so! J.

Richard read and re-read the note trying hard to make sense of it. He recognised the name Sir James, but why and in what connection, he had no idea, but he was intrigued by the comment '*of great interest to you*'.

What could be of great interest to me and why had it to be such a secret?

After what he had been through he loathed the idea of keeping any more secrets, but he was inquisitive and decided to honour the demands but with one small exception; and that was he would keep a copy of his note and pass the original to his solicitor Brian Gore for safe keeping.

Chapter 3

Richard James kissed his wife goodbye and with a confidence he hadn't displayed in a long time he got into his car and set off to Canterbury to meet the mysterious Sir James Johnstone. Sir James had arranged to meet him for dinner at the County Hotel, a comfortable four star hotel which prides itself on its cuisine, situated in the High Street right in the city centre. Richard, since receiving the handwritten note, had had mixed feelings about the meeting but as always, when it came to something shrouded in mystery, his curiosity was aroused and he just could not resist.

Perhaps I am going to be offered a peerage as recompense for what has happened!

Then reality kicked in and he thought it was probably something to do with his work as a fruit farmer.

If that's the case then why all the secrecy?

Ahead of him lay the outskirts of the city of Canterbury and not wanting to park in the County Hotel's car park he needed to concentrate on where he was going so he pushed all silly thoughts out of his head. Originally he had planned to park near the Westgate Tower and walk up St Peters Street, but then Castle Street car park was close to the County Hotel so he decided to park there. Richard made his way to the dining room of the County Hotel where he was greeted by the head waiter.

"Good evening sir, do you have a reservation this evening?" Richard glanced at his watch; it was dead on the dot of seven-thirty. *Good Sir James should be here at anytime* he thought to himself as he smiled briefly at the head waiter.

"Yes I have a table booked for 7:30 in the name of James."

"Very good sir." He scanned down his reservation sheet, "ah there it is," he looked up and smiled, "Mr James a table for two 7:30. Would you prefer to wait in the cocktail bar or will your guest join you at the table?"

"I expect that they'll be here in a minute."

"Very good sir, then if you would be kind enough to follow me I'll show you to your table." The head waiter led Richard to a table positioned away from the main body of the room and laid up ready for two. "Here we are sir. I have complied as far as possible with your request for privacy and I have had this table laid up for you. I trust that this will be suitable."

"I'm sure it will be thank you."

Richard chose the chair on the far side of the table, the one facing up the dining room as this served two purposes, one was it enabled him to see everyone else, but more to the point he could see who entered and left the dining room. Old habits die hard.

"Can I get you a drink sir?"

"Thank you, I'll have a Bushmills please?" he enquired and stole a quick look at his watch, it was now seven-forty and no sign of Sir James.

This doesn't reflect too well on your timekeeping Sir James! He picked up the menu that the head waiter had left on the table and opened it and gave a low whistle.

Well Sir James; I hope you're paying for this little lot because I'm certainly not!

"One Bushmills sir," the waiter said as he placed a cut glass whisky tumbler on the table, "oh and I have been asked to convey a message to say that your guest has arrived and that he will be with you shortly. He has also asked me to convey his apologies for his late arrival and hoped you would understand."

"Thank you."

"Not at all sir." He bobbed his head in acknowledgement and headed back to the dining room's entrance, where a tall distinguished looking gentleman with steely grey hair and impeccably dressed in a dark grey suit was waiting patiently.

"Good evening sir."

"Good evening, is Mr James here, he is expecting me?" the gentleman enquired.

"Ah yes sir, if you would kindly follow me." The head waiter led Sir James through the dining room to the lone table where Richard James was sitting.

"Good evening Richard." Sir James said as he extended his hand.

"Sir James." Richard stood up and gave a curt nod as they shook hands.

The head waiter eased the chair forward as Sir James sat down opposite Richard "I must apologise for my late arrival, but the traffic was diabolical," he said as he unfolded the napkin and placed it on his knee. "I'm pleased you decided to take me up on my offer and decided to come tonight as I have some important issues that I wish to discuss with you. Anyway Richard how are you keeping nowadays? It's been quite some time since we last met."

"Yes it has Sir James," Richard said hesitantly and smiled. *I know your face from somewhere but I'm damned if I know where,* he thought to himself. *Phew, thank goodness he didn't notice my hesitation, now where have we met?*

"Would sir care for a drink of something?" the head waiter enquired politely.

"Thank you, do you have Dalwhinnie malt?"

"Yes sir."

"A large Dalwhinnie and what about you Richard?"

"A Bushmills please."

"And a large Bushmills…"

"No, no. Just a single please as I'm driving."

"In that case, a single Bushmills for my friend and a large Dalwhinnie for me thank you."

Well Richard it seems as if your hesitancy has gone unnoticed.

Sir James waited until the head waiter was well out of earshot before speaking further.

"As I said earlier I have asked you here to discuss certain issues of grave importance and sensitivity, but before I go any further I trust you haven't divulged anything to anyone about my contacting you or about this meeting."

"I haven't breathed a word."

Well it's more or less true. I haven't said anything to anybody, except for my solicitor Brian Gore who I've asked to keep your letter as a safety precaution.

"It goes without saying that whatever we discuss tonight is highly confidential and of a very sensitive nature and I must insist on your complete discretion in this matter. You are of course still subject to the Official Secrets Act and as such are liable to certain penalties should you divulge any of what I am about to tell you to a third party. Do you accept these criteria?" Richard nodded. "Also I must add that any proposals suggested, or made, at this meeting are totally unofficial and must be regarded as such. However, I do feel that if things work out as I think they will then I'll make sure that the right people hear about it and Richard, I think once again you will be highly thought of by Her Majesty's Government."

Oh yeah! I'm sorry Sir James but I've heard it all before and where did that get me? Anyway the waiter's coming.

"I think the drinks are coming Sir James."

Sir James glanced round over his shoulder. "You're right so I'll tell you more in a moment or two."

"A large Dalwhinnie?" the waiter enquired and waited.

"Thank you." Sir James answered.

"And a Bushmills for sir."

Sir James gave him a moment or two to get well out of earshot before continuing.

"As I was saying Richard, anything we discuss tonight is totally unofficial and should you accept what I am offering it will have to remain unofficial, but trust me that's all I ask." He flashed a quick smile at Richard.

Now why should I trust you any more than the next man Sir James?

"I suppose the main question is whether you, Richard James, will be prepared to accept another challenge?" He paused and watched Richard for any reaction.

Huh, is this for you or is it for Her Majesty's Government? Once again Sir James was talking.

"You see I have the utmost faith in you, but do you have the same faith in yourself and of course in me?"

That's a good question and I am not so sure that I do at the moment Sir James but that depends on you and where we met before and under what circumstances?

Sir James had wittingly or unwittingly put Richard on the spot and as such careful thought was needed before an answer was given.

"Refresh my memory Sir James, earlier you implied, no you said and I quote 'it's been quite some time since we last met,' how long ago is it now?"

"Hmm, let me see." Sir James closed his eyes in deliberation. "I can't remember the exact date, but I think it was at Ashford." He paused for a moment or two. "Yes it was definitely Ashford. I was there; Colonel Ash and Brigadier Miles Townsend were also present, we were all there to discuss a possible operation, now what was its name?" Once more Sir James paused whilst he searched his memory for the name of the operation.

Dear me my memory's getting worse what on earth was it called? Orpus, Opus something like that. Ah yes that's it Orpheus.

"Orpheus, Operation Orpheus that was its name. You remember it don't you Richard? We were all in Ash's office and…" as Sir James prattled on about the meeting at Ashford,

Richard tried his hardest to fill in the blank gaps in his memory.

That name Orpheus, it's cropped up before somewhere but where, what has it got to do with me?

Try as he might it still wouldn't come back to him. Suddenly he realised Sir James had stopped talking and was looking at him expectantly.

"Well Richard…?"

"I'm sorry Sir James I was miles away, in fact back at the meeting in Ashford. What was it you said?"

"I asked you if you remembered that was all."

"Oh yes of course I do, sorry Sir James it's just that I've had so many meetings with different people it's sometimes hard to keep up with them all."

Not quite the truth Richard James but hopefully it will do.

Richard gave a reassuring smile and hoped Sir James believed him, after all it was partly true, he did remember Ash and he remembered bits and pieces about some operation he'd been involved with and the name Orpheus sounded familiar but that was as far as it went.

God my brain is still scrambled from being in that damned psychiatric unit.

"Good, I'm pleased we've manage to sort that out."

I sincerely hope you do remember otherwise this evening would be a complete waste of time.

"So Richard will you consider another challenge?"

Richard was silent for a minute or two as he thought over what Sir James was proposing.

Hmm, I'm not so sure Sir James not after the last episode. What reassurances can you give that will convince me that I won't get stitched up again?

"There's a saying that springs to mind, *look before you leap.* I remember jumping in with both feet last time and where did that get me, nowhere, apart from being dumped on from a great height, being harassed and then railroaded. I was double-crossed by so called friends and colleagues then thrown to the wolves. So tell me Sir James, why should I trust you anymore than the others, what's so different this time?" All the anger, the pent-up emotions and years of frustration, suddenly overflowed as Richard gave vent to his feelings, and all this time Sir James calmly sat there. His expression was impassive as he waited patiently for all the anger and frustration to subside and then he spoke.

"Richard I'll be honest with you, I know you were treated abominably by the Department and believe me had I known then what I know now then things would certainly have been different, so much so that we probably would not be sitting here now." He paused just long enough to let what he had just said sink in, "you see it is because of that poor treatment that…" The waiter's approach to the table cut him short.

"Gentlemen, are you ready to order or do you require some more time?"

"I'm sorry I haven't even looked at the menu yet. Would you give us some more time?" Sir James said as he picked up the menu.

"Certainly sir." The waiter gave a slight nod and discretely withdrew.

"As I was saying, I know how you must have suffered and I know Operation Orpheus ultimately failed. I also know about your arrest and I have a shrewd idea as to why, but let me digress a little and tell you a story." Richard listened patiently as Sir James recounted to him about other failures and how one major operation failed because somebody had inadvertently overlooked certain facts. "But nothing could be proved. This was the second or third time a major operation had failed. Now that seemed too much of a coincidence to me so I got my PA to do some fairly rudimentary checks and guess what, it didn't take her long to find that there were other operations, maybe not major ones but nonetheless equally as important, that had failed for similar reasons. In each case it appeared as if vital facts had been overlooked."

He went on to tell Richard how he initially thought it was a field operations error and had looked closely at their modus operandi, but found nothing, the information had been gathered, the information had been distributed to the correct people, everything appeared correct. "I personally interviewed some of my senior staff and they all said the same, that the information could not have been missed. It must have been there or it was tantamount to suicide. The question was, who or what was wrong, how could so many field operations fail. I knew MI6 was clean; if for no other reason than the errors we had logged were within the Military Intelligence, the errors had to be elsewhere. Then a week ago I received a call from a gentleman in the Ministry who wished to meet me. This gentleman was suggesting that err…that there were some very strange and inexplicable things happening. Operations were failing, good field operatives were being lost in mysterious circumstances and there was no longer rhyme or reason as to why these things had started to happen." Sir James paused and took a sip of his whisky.

Are you saying what I think you may be saying Sir James and that is there is a traitor or mole within the Government or Intelligence?

Sir James continued with his story and how he had arranged to meet up with Gilpin, the man from the Ministry, in Hyde Park, how Gilpin had requested help from Six – all unofficial of course. The Government, it seemed, felt that someone somewhere was leaking information to the Provisionals and the Home Office was blaming the Military, the Military was pointing the finger at MI5 and the RUC Special Branch.

"I'll be honest with you Richard, the Government has a problem, whoever he or she is they are damned clever and no matter what we do they always seem one jump ahead."

So Sir James where is all this leading to, and where does little old me fit in?

Sir James took another sip of whisky then continued to tell Richard about the Government's proposal that came to him via Mr Gilpin at the Ministry.

"I was asked if my department could help, if we had someone who would be prepared to take on the job of tracking down and identifying where the leak is."

"So why have you approached me Sir James?"

"Well…" he paused, *this is the tricky bit I just hope you will buy it Richard.* "It's like this; the Government cannot be seen to be involved in this one…"

"But if it's as you say it is then why can't they be seen to be involved?"

"Politics Richard, it's a hot potato and if the balloon went up…" He left the rest unsaid. "Anyway, suffice it to say the PM's taking an interest in this personally and has, via the man from the Ministry, enlisted my department's help in asking me if I could suggest anyone for the job. It has to be the right person, a person of high calibre and someone with the right sort of background."

Having seen your file and knowing what's happened to you, you will fit the bill admirably provided I can convince you.

"Whoever undertakes the role will be well recompensed for their efforts, and Richard having read your file I feel you have what it takes. You have certainly got the background and the tenacity to undertake this project."

I know you can do it so come on Richard grab the chance, your chance to get even.

Sir James took another sip of whisky whilst he studied Richard's face for a clue as to how his sales pitch had gone.

"I'm not sure Sir James. Once bitten twice shy so the saying goes."

"Come on Richard this is your chance don't let it slip away."

Huh, my chance to do what, drop in the shit again?

"There is one other thing you ought to know Richard…" Richard looked quizzically at Sir James. "That's what Sir James?"

"I am certain that there is a mole somewhere and I'm certain as I can be that you were set up as a scapegoat…"

Tell me something I don't already know Sir James.

"Richard someone, somewhere has manipulated the system and they sacrificed you to save themselves, not only you but many others have been sold down the river to satisfy their gratuitous ends."

Come on Richard help me to catch this bastard.

Richard opened his mouth as if to say something but closed it again. For a minute Sir James thought Richard's resolve had weakened but he was mistaken.

"Richard, help me catch this mole and I'll guarantee I'll personally help you clear your name…" Sir James waited with bated breath whilst Richard mulled over what had been said. He took a mouthful of Bushmills whilst he thought about the proposition.

It is certainly tempting, and Paul and I have already talked along similar lines but I don't know. One minute Her Majesty's Government is busy stitching me up and in the next they are asking for my help. He was in two minds. *Be cautious Richard, be cautious. How can you trust them again after what happened before? On the other hand here's a golden opportunity to get even, provided you and the family get full protection and certain guarantees.*

He took another sip of Bushmills. He couldn't help feeling flattered to think that Sir James had singled him out from all the other people that he could have used and that he also had ultimate trust in his capabilities. All this time Sir James sat patiently waiting for his answer.

"One question Sir James."

"Fire away."

"The proposed payment and what about my past?" asked Richard.

"That's two questions, but let me deal with the simple one first, the payment. Of course you will be paid but as this post is unofficial in reality you and the post don't exist! However you will be given expenses…"

"What…" Richard interjected.

Sir James held up his hand.

"Hear me out Richard, by giving you expenses all that means is that your name does not appear on any Government payroll. You are invisible and that way nobody knows you exist so you retain your anonymity. Of course the expenses will reflect your true worth and there will be an extra sum involved for, shall we say cost of living! As a total I had in mind around forty to forty-five, but what do you think?"

"Forty to forty-five pounds a week, bah, you must be joking!"

"Not forty to forty-five pounds a week, but forty to forty-five thousand a year plus your cost of living allowance. Let's say it's a thousand a week, how does that sound?"

"It's OK but nothing special when you think that when I worked for O'Shea back in the 1970s I was earning good money."

"Richard I know exactly what you earned with O'Shea back in the 1970s. Don't forget I have access to everything about you and back then you paid tax on that money. As this sum is down to expenses it can be *arranged* that it is tax free so that will mean you will be earning the equivalent to sixty-five thousand plus a year before tax, that's over twelve hundred a week. Now are you interested?"

"Depends..."

"On what?"

"On what you can do regarding my army pension which has been frozen, I want that reinstated."

"That can be sorted out. Is there anything else?"
Richard now felt he was in the driving seat and started to push hard.

"Yes, there's the little matter of protection."

"Protection!" Sir James looked puzzled, "how do you mean?"

"My family's protection and my protection should anything go wrong. Also there's the little point of giving me back my life that the Government stole from me." There was a fleeting look of concern from Sir James as Richard mentioned the last item, but it went just as quickly as it had appeared.

"You say you would like protection for you and your family should things go wrong. Now do you mean financial or physical?"

"Both. For instance if things do go wrong I want some form of redress in the financial sense and I want physical protection for my family against any reprisals that may happen. A new life, a new home and a new identity, that should do for starters."

"I see." Sir James fell silent for a moment whilst he thought over what Richard had just said. "The physical protection, the change of identity, a new life and home somewhere even abroad if needs must is not a problem; after all we do that all the time for witness protection, as for the financial side, that's a little trickier." Sir James looked serious for a time as he tried to figure out how to give Richard what he wanted. Suddenly a grin lightened his whole countenance. "How about if we set up a good insurance policy, something along the lines of an endowment policy on you and your family with a whole life section and a 'with profits' section. The whole life section would be payable on death and the 'with profits' section would be payable upon retirement. I think that would more than answer what you're looking for." It certainly sounded good in principle but Richard couldn't help thinking everything had been just a little too easy and this made him suspicious.

"Where's the catch?" he asked.

"No catch, it's a straight forward insurance policy paid for by us which will also give you a pension."

It all sounds too good to be true but go for it and see what happens!

"OK," he said but his voice had a note of reservation in it which Sir James chose to overlook.

"Now about 'giving you back the life that the Government stole' as you put it, that's a little trickier. However what I can do is to persuade the powers that be to do something about your medical records so that there is no mention there about you being sectioned or treated at Chartham. As for your credit rating, that's no problem. That can be fixed within the department. Of course your assets that were frozen have already been released and we can of course delete any record of that ever happening. Oh, I almost forgot. Your Police record, I've had that pulled and I must say I couldn't find any reference to enquiries into Richard James or any records held on Richard James." Sir James gave a sly wink and took a drink. "Ah that's a nice drop of whisky." He put down his tumbler and lightly dabbed his lips with his napkin before continuing, "so you see I have already started giving you your life back!"

Richard thought about the conversation and what Sir James had done already and he had to admit, having weighed up the pros and cons, Sir James had been exceedingly fair.

"I must say that I am impressed but there is one very minor thing I haven't asked?"

"Oh and what's that Richard?"

"Why me?"

"A good question. Let's just say I recognise a good operator when I see one and I'm convinced with your tenacity and based on the reports I have had about you I am convinced that if anyone can find our mole you can. Does that answer your question?"

"Yes Sir James."

"In that case let's order our meal."

Chapter 4

There was a definite spring in Richard's step as he walked back to his car; it was as if a great weight had been removed from his shoulders and Sir James was the one person who had managed to give him the incentive he needed, the incentive to establish his innocence and suddenly the world was a better place. At last, someone now had faith and believed in him, and *tonight* was the start of the rest of his life.

He couldn't help feeling more than just a little pleased with himself as he started his car and turned left out of the car park to join Rheims Way and head for home. However, it wasn't long before the flush of euphoria was replaced by the harsh realism of the situation and the truth was that he was on his own.

There was no back up for him this time should things go tits up. No safety net and no real team, just figures in the shadows and now he had to differentiate between friendly shadows and the enemy.

The more he thought about it the more futile the task seemed. Again nagging doubts started to gnaw at his confidence and he began to wonder if he had done the right thing.

Should he have ignored the letter from Sir James and just gone with the original idea, just him and Paul trying to piece together a jigsaw? On the other hand he will have a reasonable income that will certainly help in financing his personal agenda to clear his name. If Sir James is to be trusted then not only would he be able to prove his innocence with pay, he will also trap an informer.

All these thoughts tumbled around in his head like washing in a tumble dryer – there was no easy option or answer for that matter. As he turned onto the London bound carriageway of the A2 he decided that instead of going home he would go straight to Paul's house and tell him the questionable good news, and then a thought struck him like a bolt of lightning.

What if the leak was from Paul?

He hadn't even considered that option and the very fact that he was considering it now caused a sharp intake of breath.

No that idea is preposterous.

Nevertheless it was still a possibility and had to be considered.

Damn it, how ridiculous can you get Richard James? You've known Paul all these years, he would never betray you!

But already doubts were creeping in. He pushed these demons to the back of his mind and tried to think more positively.

But supposing it is him? You need to consider it as a possibility. The voice in his head said.

"I know, I know" he shouted out loud as he turned off the main road and headed towards Paul's place and it was in that instant he knew exactly what had to be done.

Opposite the entrance to the small housing estate where Paul lived was a pull-in. Richard slowed the car but instead of indicating to turn right into the housing estate he pulled into the lay-by and parked. Although it was important that he talked to Paul, it was much more important that he had his trust. After considering all the options open to him Richard felt the best way forward was to say nothing about the meeting with Sir James and that way it would seem as if he was going with the original idea that he and Paul had already discussed, all he needed now was a plan of action.

He had now been parked for the best part of a quarter of an hour and was still no nearer to a solution than when he first stopped. Oh he had had plenty of thoughts on the subject but one way or another he had to discard them all, then out of the blue it came to him.

Of course, the plan was so simple, why hadn't it occurred to him before?

He would sit down with Paul and suggest they start with the unit that they were training as a 'snatch' squad. It would mean putting each and every man under the microscope, but that wouldn't be too difficult, after all they already had suspicions about George Imanos albeit they were unproven.

If only there was a link between him and someone else then we could follow that link.

The beginning of an idea began to germinate and operation codenamed *'Beggarman'* was up and running.

Yes that was it; Paul to investigate Imanos, his contacts and anybody else in Kent such as Johnny Rains, and I'll look at the contacts in Ireland.

With this uppermost in his mind Richard started the engine of the car and set off to Paul's.

As he turned into The Crescent, Paul's house came into view on the left.

Well this is it. Here goes with round one.

As he pulled up outside the house he was relieved to see a light was still on in the sitting-room indicating that Paul was still up.

The front door to Paul's house was typical of the houses on this small estate, a solid wood door, the solid frame forming a surround for four equally spaced wooden panels. Although it couldn't been seen at night there was a small but neatly laid out front garden that comprised of a small area of lawn edged with flower beds. Richard pressed the bell push and winced as the electronic door chimes played their tacky musical notes. Before the last note had played Paul opened the door.

"Hi Richard, what brings you here at this time?"

"Well I've been thinking about things…"

"Come in mate." Richard followed Paul into his lounge, "I was just about to go to bed."

"I'm sorry Paul, I didn't realise. I'll come back tomorrow." Richard turned as if to go but secretly hoped Paul's curiosity would get the better of him and he was right.

"Whoa, not so fast, it'll keep. So tell me what's up?"

"Are you sure?" Richard asked hoping that the concern in his voice sounded genuine. "As I said I can come back in the morning if it's inconvenient. It'll keep." But all the time hoping that Paul would bite and he wasn't disappointed.

"No, no stay. It's no problem. Sit down and I'll make us a coffee."

Yes! I knew I could rely on your insatiable curiosity and I was right.

"So what do you want to talk about?" Paul called from the kitchen.

"I've been thinking things over…"

"And…"

"You know you said you would help me prove I was stitched up…"

"Yeah…"

"Well I've decided to follow it up."

"Oh and how?"

"Well I have this idea but I need your input as well."

There was silence, and for a moment Richard thought that may be it wasn't such a good idea after all. He called to Paul again, trying a slightly different approach.

"Of course, if you prefer, I could wait until the morning." Richard metaphorically speaking held his breath. Then it came, the response he had hoped for.

"No way. You've started something so let's be having it tonight." A couple of seconds later, Paul appeared with two steaming mugs of coffee.

"Well I had this idea that maybe just maybe there was a 'traitor' or 'spy' in our midst."

"Well that's original." Paul said sarcastically, "We know there was, it was Rains who bubbled us to the Police."

"No I mean before then. I'm talking way back, way back in Ireland."

"Like how far back? Are you talking as far back as the time with O'Shea?"

"Could be, but I don't think so, all the same I can't discount it. I think it certainly goes back to when I worked up in Ulster."

"Why do you say that?"

"I don't know it's just a gut feeling."

Sir James had said, 'Richard someone, somewhere has manipulated the system and they sacrificed you to save themselves, not only you but many others have been sold down the river to satisfy their gratuitous ends.'

"I can't prove anything but odd things happened."

"Such as…?"

Richard talked to Paul about his concerns and about the different things that had happened to both of them. He told him about Sean O'Donald's murder, and how someone had attempted to murder Jean O'Donald by pushing her BMW off the road whilst she was driving back from a 'business' meeting. He told Paul a number of things that previously he had never known about, like the catastrophic failure of the operation aimed at lifting Riley. The killing of Wyman's car driver by a car bomb outside the safe house. The Provisionals attack on the safe house in the province. All these and many other incidents he cited in order to convince Paul that there was a definite threat from 'within', and that a mole existed, but Paul remained sceptical especially when it came to their arrest and he certainly made no bones about it.

"You must be joking Richard. Our arrest was triggered by that pillock John Rains who reported us to the Police and as for the other incidents you've talked about – well, what can I say other than what's already been said. For instance Sean

O'Donald, you told me yourself it was Riley's boys who planted the explosive device that killed him. As for the abortive attempt of grabbing Riley that was bad information – poor communication, call it what you will, and again this was by your own admission. So where's this 'mole' or 'traitor' you're on about – bah I'll tell you where, it's in your head, it's in your imagination that's where." Having delivered such a blistering attack Paul the fell into a sullen silence and Richard carefully considered his next move before speaking. He needed Paul to see sense and to get him on his side so he thought long and hard. Then he came up with an idea.

I'll challenge your trustworthiness; yes that's what I'll do.
Richard had known Paul for many years, they went all the way back to childhood days and he knew most of his little quirks and foibles. For instance he knew that if he questioned Paul's integrity then his first reaction would be to laugh, treating it as a joke. But he also knew that if he appeared to be adamant in questioning Paul's integrity, then Paul would become quite indignant and immediately set out to prove that his friend was wrong. Richard knew he would win and reacted accordingly.

"I hear what you are saying Paul, but can't you see it. Make everything look coincidental and you've got the best cover-up going. Yes, our arrest was because John Rains reported us to the Police, and I accept that but I've spent months and months reliving each event and do you know Paul, I'm even more convinced that there was a traitor or a mole in the operation. I even considered you as a possibility…"

"What! You must be joking…" Paul replied indignantly, and then true to form started to laugh at such a preposterous idea.

"Well you must admit you were closer to me than anyone else, and what's more you knew what was going on so it's not inconceivable is it?" Richard continued in the same vein.

"Thanks pal for your vote of confidence." Paul answered in a derisory fashion then fell silent feigning mock hurt. He then realised that Richard wasn't smiling.

Hang on I'm your friend in all this.

"You're not serious are you?" Paul asked quietly. Richard didn't reply.

Yes Paul I know you so well! A couple of seconds more should do the trick.

"Hey Richard, you are serious aren't you!" Paul exclaimed and fell silent.

Come on Richard this is crap and you know it is.

"Don't be such a pillock Richard. It's me Paul you're talking about not some oddball two-bit individual. I'm your best mate." Paul retorted angrily. The anger and hurt at his integrity being brought into question by his long-term friend was written all over his face.

Bingo! Mr Jones I do know you and my assessment was right, you actually believed me when I said I considered it to be you.

Inwardly Richard allowed a little smile in self gratification for being able to psyche out his old friend. He now let the trace of a smile touch the corners of his mouth.

"No not really" he answered. "Anyway, it couldn't be you because you knew nothing about what I was doing over in Ulster. All right you knew Sean but you didn't know about the operation to grab Riley nor did you know about the attempt on Jean O'Donald's life. As for our arrest, well as you say, it was Johnny Rains who told the Police so I can't even blame you for that one," Richard grinned. "No mate I don't think it's you."

Paul inwardly kicked himself knowing that he had been outsmarted by his friend, but was also pleased to know that in truth Richard had never doubted him. "Shit Richard, for a minute there I thought you were serious…"

"Oh I was," he interrupted him, "I was actually considering you at one stage, but as I have said there is nothing to link you. No what we need to do is to find some common link, and what's more we need proof."

"So you are serious about there being a traitor or mole?"

"Oh yes, I'm serious all right. I've never been more serious in my whole life." The tone of Richard's voice underlined his determination and it didn't take Paul long to appreciate the gravity of what he had just said.

"Hmm. So where do you propose we start?" Paul asked.

"I'm not too sure, but I think the only way we can get anywhere is by looking closely at what has happened over the years and who the key players have been."

"Perhaps we ought to start with those in the unit."

"That's exactly my feelings. Now who would you say are the main players?"

"Well there's Imanos and Rains."

"OK so what's their connection?"

"Both in the unit and Rains admitted to blowing the whistle on us."

"So Rains blows the whistle, but how does that connect with Imanos?"

"Hmm, I don't know is the simple answer."

"Exactly, so we need to think this through and besides, the arrest wasn't the problem it was what followed that was the problem."

"How do you mean?"

"Well the Police trying to put you in the frame for a murder you didn't do. Then the fact that you were at GCHQ and there was a cover up by a Government department that very nearly got you banged up. The fact that I was removed to a psychiatric unit on some trumped up charge, the fact that my phone was tapped and the gypsy's warning by the heavy mob, all these sorts of things, the list is never ending."

"I see what you mean now. Come to think of it I'd forgotten all about the GCHQ affair and you're right there are a lot of unexplained happenings."

At last Paul was convinced and Richard heaved an inward sigh of relief. So it was agreed, Paul would concentrate his time and effort in Kent whilst Richard went back to Ireland, for it was there that Richard felt the answer or answers lay. Deep down he knew that if he could uncover who the person was that used him as a scapegoat then he would have found the mole.

The owner of the Evinrude Hotel was a man in his late forties, about 5'10" and of broad physique. He had cropped dark brown hair and eyes as dark as coal. His top lip was covered with a large bushy moustache. In all, his countenance was of swarthy appearance and quite intimidating. He always kept himself fit and followed a strict regime of a daily workout at the gym, Yes, George Imanos was in remarkable shape for his age. He seemed to be very much of a loner and with few friends with the exception of one person in whose company he had been frequently seen, a man by the name of Lamar. Lamar was a strange individual; he constantly wore dark glasses and had shoulder length hair, not the type one would readily connect with Imanos. George Imanos would introduce Lamar as a colleague or an acquaintance depending on who he was with at the time. He would never ever suggest, or for that matter, introduce Lamar as a friend.

The phone in the reception rang three or four times before Imanos picked it up.

"The Evinrude Hotel" George answered in a disinterested monotone.

"James is back into society," a low, softly spoken voice at the other end of the line announced. "Both Lamar and I saw him the other week" the voice continued, "and the boss needs to know what he and Jones are up to, so your orders are to set up a surveillance team urgently and report back. We don't want him querying our pitch do we?" He didn't wait for Imanos to answer but continued talking, "So do whatever is necessary, even to the point of persuading our old friend Rains to help." The voice had changed. It was no longer soft; it was now dark and menacing. "Do not forget his son is still on a tour of duty in Ulster, so perhaps he could be persuaded to help in some way. Arrange it." The voice snapped down the line. The owner of the voice didn't wait for Imanos to reply, there was a click as whoever it was put down the phone. The line went dead. Imanos frowned at first as if puzzled by the phone call, but his frown was quickly replaced by a thoughtful expression.

It had been some little while since Imanos had received the telephone call advising him that Richard James was back in circulation and since then he had been busy making plans. He now picked up the phone to put his plan into action.

"Dave, George here. My firm has a small job for your company. A bloke called Rains, lives in Surrey Road Cliftonville. I need you to speak to him, persuade him that for the good of his family, and in particular his son, he needs to co-operate. Tell him that this is vital for the country's security and in his best interest. Make it look and sound official. You will no doubt be overpaid once again!" With that little quip he replaced the handset.

Paul replaced the receiver and glanced at his watch. He decided that he had just about enough time to grab a bite of something to eat before leaving to meet up with Johnny Rains for a drink. John Rains was the man who had told Paul and Richard about George Imanos being connected with the Irish Republican Socialist Party (IRSP) and being in cahoots with Lamar, another member of the IRSP, so Paul felt that a social drink and a chat about old times may well be useful and he had high hopes of finding out something from his forthcoming meeting.

It was just after eight thirty as John Rains left his house in Surrey Road Margate and got into a green Vauxhall Cavalier parked outside the gate. The engine turned over a couple of times then kicked into life. He checked his rear view mirror for on-coming vehicles before indicating to move off.

Ok Johnny, all's clear except for that red Sierra that's just pulling out up the road but you've got plenty of time to get out. Slowly he moved off up the road.

G517OKP.

Sub-consciously he made a mental note of the red Sierra's registration number, old habits die hard, he then realised what he had done.

I don't know Johnny Rains; it's got to be sad when you automatically take note of car registrations. Time you gave up being a Traffic Warden.

Had he been a little more observant then he would have realised that the innocent looking red Sierra, which had set off at the same time, was actually following him. Unfortunately Johnny Rains wasn't suspicious by nature, nor had he been trained to be that observant!

The Eight Bells was a sixteenth century coaching inn hidden away from prying eyes down a narrow country lane in the hamlet of Wingham Well. It oozed ambience with plenty of oak beams and a large open inglenook fireplace. The place was steeped in history and was, what the Americans would call, quaint and full of character. Being off the beaten track and midway between Canterbury and Cliftonville made it the ideal venue for what Paul had in mind and dead on the dot of nine o'clock he settled down to await the arrival of John Rains.

Just after nine fifteen John Rains turned off the narrow country lane into the car park belonging to the Eight Bells and parked his car as close as he could to the door of the pub. As he shut and locked the car door he could smell the faint aroma of burning apple wood wafting on the night air. A small gust of wind whipped odd bits of litter into a mini vortex, it grabbed at his jacket and tugged his hair but then it was gone to be replaced by a gentle breeze which caressed his face and plucked at his hair as he walked the short distance to the pub. As he pushed open the door a red Sierra swung into the car park and slowed to a halt at the far end where the driver manoeuvred the car into a position where he had a clear view of all the building and its entrances.

As John Rains entered the main bar he heard a familiar voice greeting his arrival,

"Hello John pleased to see you again." He swung round to see his old Sergeant Major Paul Jones as he came towards him hand outstretched. "What will you have to drink?" Paul enquired as he shook Johnny Rains by the hand.

"A small bitter please. How are you keeping Paul?"

"Fine and yourself?"

"Oh, not too bad. How's Richard?"

"He's all right. If you go and sit over there," Paul indicated the table he had been sitting at, "I'll get your beer in."

John hadn't been sitting long before Paul returned with a glass of beer. "So what have you been up to John, are you still dishing out tickets?"

"Yes I'm afraid I'm still working as a traffic warden, a yellow peril as the saying goes."

"So is the yellow band around the hat to stop people parking on your head?"

John smiled politely. "Ha, ha very droll Paul. I see your sense of humour hasn't changed, it's still as bad as ever."

"I know, terrible isn't it but I bet you miss it all the same? You know it's a long time since we've spoken. In fact the last time was the night before Richard and I were arrested." Paul watched to see if his last comment got any reaction.

"Ah yes." John gave a slight sigh, "the same night that I came to both you and Richard to tell you about Imanos and co., but you wouldn't listen."

For a long time now he had wanted to apologise to Paul and Richard for what he had done but had never really had the courage to do so.

Now that Paul had mentioned it he saw this as an opportunity to get it off his chest.

"I'm sorry about the arrest but it was the only way I could think of stopping you from going on what was tantamount to being a suicide mission, more to the point, it was the only way I could see of my getting out of it. If only you and Richard had listened to me and taken notice of what I was saying then I wouldn't have gone to the Police and you wouldn't have been arrested. All I can do now is apologise for my actions and hope you understand why I did what I did. As it's now in the past, it's dead and buried so don't you think it's better forgotten Paul?" With that out of the way, Johnny Rains felt as if a great weight had, once and for all, been lifted from his shoulders.

"Hmm." Paul took his time to think through what John had just told him, but in the end had to accept that what was done was done and no amount of recriminations would change anything. "I guess you're right, so here's to you John, cheers," he picked up his glass and took two or three mouthfuls of beer.

"Cheers Paul and here's to you and Richard."

At that precise moment a blast of cool night air was felt as the outside door was opened and two young men entered, and like many village pubs conversation momentarily ceased whilst those present gave the newcomers a cursory look over. The two strangers paused and glanced around and with a muttered 'good evening' and cursory nod of the head to those closest, they moved to the bar where they ordered their drinks. In a matter of seconds and a few muttered 'good evenings' in response the general hubbub in the room returned.

Throughout the evening Paul and John chatted about old times and what they had been doing since that fateful day of the arrest. They talked about Johnny's son and his tour of duty in Ulster. They spoke about how Johnny had found out about Imanos and how he had links with the IRSP in the Republic, and all the time they talked, the two young men moved closer mingling with those around them. In fact unnoticed by Paul and John the two young men had now moved over to the fruit machine adjacent to where they were sitting and well within earshot. Yes all the time Paul and John Rains talked the two young men were close by!

"Well Paul thanks for this evening but it's time I made a move. By the way, where's Richard tonight, you never did say what had happened to him?"

"Oh, didn't I tell you? Well he's planning on going over to Ireland, you see after the arrest things went slightly pear shaped so ... well it wasn't a good time."

"Oh" Johnny Rains looked puzzled, "in what way?"

"Well things didn't go according to plan; let's just leave it at that."

"OK. Anyway once again thank you for the chat Paul and keep in touch. I'd better get off." He extended an outstretched hand towards Paul who immediately shook it.

"Yeah I will. See you Johnny." With that Johnny and Paul parted company, Paul headed off to the toilets as Johnny went out of the door. Had Paul stayed he would not have failed to notice the two young men suddenly leave their drinks and make a hurried exit behind Johnny Rains.

Johnny Rains was vaguely aware of someone's approach as he took the car keys from his pocket. Then suddenly he felt a thud as someone or something solid hit him from behind. The next thing he realised was that he was being bundled into a car - then blackness.

He wasn't sure how long he had been unconscious or for that matter what the time was, all he knew was that he awoke with a thumping headache gagged and blindfolded by means of a hood pulled tightly down over his head. His arms had been pulled behind him and his wrists were tightly bound.

"Now you be listening, and listen good because I'll only say this once. Nod your head to let me know you understand or shake your head to let me know you don't. Do you understand?" Johnny Rains nodded his head. "Good. Then this is the deal. We have been watching your wife, your daughter in-law and grandchildren. Your son is in Ulster and unless you do as we say his photograph will appear in every newspaper in the country and his description, now you wouldn't want anything like that to happen would you, do you understand?"
Once more he nodded his head. "Good then this is what you have to do. Tomorrow you will visit your friend Mr Jones and you will endeavour to find out what he and his mate James are up to." Then his voice sounded more menacing as he said, "don't forget we know where you live and all about your family. Now you wouldn't want them to come to any harm would you, you do of course understand don't you?" Johnny nodded his head. "Well, do as you're told and everything will be fine, after all it's in your interest and the security of our country is paramount. Understood?" Once again he nodded his head. "So tomorrow you visit Jones and find out what he and James are up to. You'll record every word on this." The owner of the voice then thrust something roughly into John's pocket. "You will then wrap the recorder up in newspaper and place the package in the litter bin on Northdown Road near the parade of shops. Is that understood?" Johnny gave the

obligatory nod of his head. "Right you are now clear on what to do. Oh there is one more thing, do not go to the Police as this is official and is bigger than you think. Do I make myself clear?" Again Johnny nodded. He was certainly convinced that they meant what they said and that by some freak accident he had got himself embroiled into some sort of Government operation.

What was it about Jones and James that attracted the interest of people in high places?

"Right Mr Rains we are now going to drive you a short distance and we will then untie your hands and set you free. You will not breathe a word about this to a soul understood?" Again Johnny nodded his head and at that precise instant the car's engine kicked into life and he felt it move off.

How many of them are there, two or is there more, he wasn't sure but there was definitely more than one.

The car bumped and jolted as it moved slowly along what Johnny assumed was a cart track then the ride was much smoother. The car accelerated quickly but it only seemed to last for a few minutes before the occupants were once again being jolted and bounced around for a second time as they travelled across more rough terrain then they stopped. Johnny felt the bonds around his wrists being pulled so tight that they cut into the skin. Then he felt a sawing sensation as a knife or something cut into them and suddenly his hands were free. His immediate thought was to make a grab for one of his captors but before he had a chance the car door was opened and he was bundled out onto the ground and the door slammed shut again as the car drove off at high speed. He struggled to his feet grappling with the hood as he did so in a vain attempt to get the car's registration, but too late, his captors were gone. He pulled the gag from his mouth and gulped in the cool fresh night air. He seemed to be on some sort of road surface with trees either side but exactly where he had no idea. In the distance he could hear the sound of an approaching car and suddenly it was upon him, the light from its headlights, broken up by bushes and small trees, spilled into where he was as it swept by. He was in some sort of lay-by. Having got his bearings he walked in the direction from which the headlights had first appeared and very soon he was out of the lay-by and onto the road. He could quite clearly hear the sound of traffic in the distance and then realisation dawned; he was a mere couple of hundred yards from the pub car park where he had been earlier that night.

It didn't take long to reach the car park where he had left his car and to his surprise the pub was still open. For the first time there was enough light to enable him to see the time and to his surprise the whole episode of him being grabbed, threatened and then dumped in the lay-by had all taken place in the space of just a little over an hour. Seeing the pub was still open he toyed with the idea of going in to raise the alarm, but then the words of his captors still rang loud in his ears.

'Don't forget we know where you live and all about your family. Now you wouldn't want them to come to any harm would you?'

He decided that perhaps that would not be so wise after all. To his surprise even his car was still there with the keys in the driver's door lock.

At last the woozy feeling and the nauseous pain in his head was beginning to subside and he was able to think more clearly. Who were his captors and where had they come from? Were they something to do with the Government, because that's the way they were talking? What was it they said, he tried to recall the actual words spoken. He remembered something about security being paramount. No that wasn't it, "Ah got it," he called out loud without realising. Then he felt embarrassed in case someone had heard him and thought he had gone crackers. He looked around, but he was alone, no cause for concern. Yes that was it, he thought to himself, the expression they used was *'this is official and is bigger than you think'* inferring it was something to do with the British Government. He thrust his hand into his jacket pocket and removed a small rectangular object. "So that's what it is," he muttered to himself as he examined the small battery operated dictaphone in his hand.

Two miles away a red Ford Sierra had stopped alongside a call box in the village of Wingham in order that the passenger, a young man in his late twenties to early thirties, could make a quick call.

"It's Carl speaking. Is that you Imanos?"

"Yes." A voice answered at the end of the line. "So what have you got?"

"The target moved out tonight. Followed him to the Eight Bells at Wingham Well where he met with second guy. Target called him Paul so we assume it was Jones. He also referred to Richard. We put the frighteners on him and suggested that he should make a visit as requested. What was that? Yes of course, yes he has the tape and I'm sure he'll oblige especially in light of what we suggested would happen if he didn't."

"Are you certain?" Imanos asked.

"Sure I'm certain, he thinks that it's the Government and that if he doesn't comply his son and family will be in grave danger, so I'm certain."

"Good. Well done lads and let me know as soon as he has performed tomorrow."

It was eleven fifteen by the time John Rains got home to Cliftonville. He entered his house in Surrey Road and ran up the stairs taking them two at a time. Not quite sure what to expect when he got to his bedroom, he paused outside. Then to his great relief his wife's sleepy voice called to him from the darkness of the room.

"Is that you John?"

He heaved an inward sigh of relief, she was safe.

Thank God for that.

"Yes I'm home," he replied, "I won't be a minute." He listened intently and through the stillness and quiet of the house he could just about hear his beloved wife breathing gently as she went back to sleep.

Suddenly the silence was shattered by the strident ring of the telephone Johnny rushed into the bedroom and grabbed the handset. His blood ran cold as he recognised the voice.

"Remember what we said Johnny…Remember your son in Ulster…Remember that we know where you live…Visit Jones tomorrow…OK?" His wife stirred.

"Who is it?" she asked in a sleepy voice.

Johnny covered the mouthpiece.

"No-one love, go back to sleep," he said hoping his voice didn't betray the fear inside him. His wife moved and turned over and quickly went back to sleep. With his heart pounding deep inside his chest he heard the voice again calling his name. It repeated again what it said a couple of seconds before.

"Remember what we said Johnny…Remember your son in Ulster…Remember that we know where you live…Visit Jones tomorrow…OK?" Now he uncovered the mouthpiece. Now he spoke in a desperate half whisper in case his wife heard.

"I don't believe what you said." He hoped his voice sounded convincing even though he didn't feel convinced.

"Can you really afford not to believe us Johnny?" There was a veiled threat hidden in the question. A certain menace in the tone of the voice, just enough of an edge to it to make him think that perhaps he ought not to be too hasty. He hesitated for a moment or two longer. Again the voice spoke in his ear. Again the veiled threat in the question. "Are you sure you can afford the luxury of not believing Johnny? Remember you son." In the end his nerve went and Johnny buckled.

"OK, OK. I'll do it.' He half whispered and half spat the words down the phone. "Just leave my family alone," was all he said.

"Well done Johnny" the voice said, "I will wait for tomorrow with interest."

Before Johnny could answer the line went dead. His shoulders slumped as he slowly lowered the handset. He felt a defeated man. He was angry with himself. Angry with them but it was out of his hands now. He sat and stared at the phone in his hand then slowly he replaced the receiver.

His wife stirred and opened her eyes. "What time is it darling?"

He looked at his watch. "Just after quarter past eleven," he said and smiled at her.

"I love you John Rains."

He leaned down and kissed her gently. "And I love you too" he whispered, "I love you too."

Imanos shut the door to his office, switched on the cassette recorder and listened intently to the muffled voices. He heard who he assumed to be Paul Jones, say something about Richard James visiting Ireland, but a lot of the conversation he couldn't make out because of the poor quality of the recording. In the end all he could say with certainty was that Richard James was going back to Ireland, as to when he couldn't be sure but he assumed it was in the near future. The only other thing the recording threw up was that he was going on his own, and that was unusual. Imanos knew Jones had a small engineering business in the Faversham area, and he knew that he had a staff working for him, so why wasn't he going? He pondered on this conundrum for some time but still he couldn't figure out why.

In the end he decided that a visit from some of Lamar's friends may well give him the answer.

Paul was used to people dropping in on an evening to discuss different jobs, it had happened more times than he cared to remember, so he wasn't unduly perturbed when the small metal door into his workshop opened and three strangers walked in and headed over to where he was working.

"Can I help you?" he asked them but they didn't reply. "Is it a job you want doing?" Still they didn't speak. Paul began to feel uneasy.

These guys were up to no good.

His mind switched into overdrive and suddenly his whole body became tense, waiting to see who was going to make the first move. There was a glint from something in the hand of the one in the middle. There was flash of cold steel as he lunged towards Paul. Instinctively he sidestepped and parried, deflecting the knife away, grabbing his assailant's lead arm as he did so. He forced the arm back and down, and then with a sudden upwards thrust and a twist of his body, he lifted his attacker off his feet by using his knife arm as a lever. There was a nauseating crack as the arm snapped like a stick and a metallic clatter as the knife fell to the floor. The man screamed in agony as he pivoted about his now shattered arm, and lifted skywards to land with a sickening thud against the wall. Knocked unconscious by the impact, he slithered to the floor where he lay motionless. Anyone could see from the grotesque position of his wrist and arm that he needed urgent hospital attention. One of his mates made a grab at Paul but like the first one he was too slow and grappled at fresh air. Paul grabbed a twelve inch length of steel rod that lay close at hand and used this as a weapon.

The man recovered and turned quickly. Too late he realised his mistake. He felt the pain as Paul landed the blow. A blinding flash of light exploded in his head then darkness. Paul turned to tackle the last of the trio but he was already heading towards the door. He had seen enough and wasn't hanging around to end up like his mates. With the last one gone Paul turned his attention to the two in the workshop, but a quick search of the blood soaked clothes did not reveal anything to him. No name, no wallet, no money. In fact there was nothing to give him any clues as to who they were or where they were from. A low moan came from attacker number two as he gradually came round. He gingerly raised a hand to his nose which seemed to be the epicentre of his pain. It felt warm and sticky on his fingers and even the lightest touch brought excruciating pain. He pulled his hand away sharply and stared at it as if trying to comprehend why there was so much blood. Slowly his head cleared and he looked around the workshop, saw Paul and the memories flooded back.

"Ah so you are back in the land of the living." Paul's tone hardened. "Right sunshine, talk and talk fast. Who sent you?" He waited for a reply.

Broken-nose scrabbled to get up. There was another explosion of pain as Paul's booted foot landed square to his ribs.

"I asked you a question. Who sent you and your mates?" He didn't answer. A low moan from the crumpled heap over by the wall immediately attracted Paul's attention; the first attacker was coming round. The second one, having now fully recovered, saw his chance and before Paul realised he was on his feet and running like a frightened rabbit towards the door.

"Come here." Paul's shout echoed after him.

"Fuck you," he shouted and was gone. Paul now turned his attention to the first attacker, who by now had struggled to his feet. "So who sent you and your mates?" The guy just looked at him in a forlorn sort of way and shook his head.

You're not going to get any sense out him, Paul thought to himself. "I'll tell you now sunshine, you had best piss off back to where you crawled from," Paul said pointing toward the door, "and don't come back here again." The last one of the three, oblivious to any pain, half staggered and half ran through the workshop and out into the darkness beyond.

Time to call Richard and tell him things are warming up!

Richard, upon receiving Paul's telephone call about his unwelcome guests, decides that now is the time for him to return to Ireland, and within seven days he is booked on the ferry to Dublin.

Chapter 5

As the ferry entered the harbour it was like a homecoming. The noise of the vehicle engines starting and the smell of diesel heavy in the air from the engine room brought fond memories flooding back. He wondered what had happened to Fionnuala, had she eventually got married and settled down to family life, or was she still working at the Tara? He had completely lost touch with her after his incarceration. The engine of his car roared into life and he joined the queue of disembarking vehicles as they moved slowly towards the ramp. The line of traffic gradually spewed out onto the dockside and within ten minutes he was heading towards the exit and out onto the main road.

The man in the white Volvo seemed totally disinterested as he sat there watching the vehicles from the ferry trundle past on their way out of the docks. That was until he noticed the blue Renault 21 emerge from the bowels of the ferry, then suddenly he was very interested, yes very interested indeed. The last time he had seen that car was when he had been over in the UK, now what would Richard James be up to over here. He hadn't heard anything officially or unofficially through his sister Fionnuala. In fact his sister hadn't heard from Richard for over two years. Danny watched as the Renault 21 drove passed him, waited for another couple of cars, then pulled out into the stream of traffic and started to follow him. As the cars left the dock area the Renault turned onto the road heading north towards Swords and he did the same.

Richard quickly glanced in his rear view mirror and subconsciously checked out the vehicles behind because in his game old habits die hard. He did not notice anything odd as he turned north towards Swords. The plan was to pay Rosie, one of his old contacts, a social call and see if he could glean any information from her. He was banking on the fact that, being near Dublin and a contact that was rarely used, the department may well have failed to inform her of his fall from glory. Again he glanced up at the mirror. Funny he thought, as he carried on at a leisurely pace towards his destination, that white Volvo has been there for a while now.

He reached down and turned on the radio for a bit of company just in time to catch the news on BBC World Service. There had been another night of violence in Ulster. A plane had crashed killing a number of people and the cold war was still very chilly. He decided the news was depressing so retuned the radio looking for some music. Again he glanced up at the mirror, the Volvo was still there. A frown creased his brow, was it following him he wondered? There was only one way to find out. With that he changed down into third, floored the accelerator, the engine roared and the rev counter reached the red line. Changed into fourth and redlined again. Changed into fifth, the engine settled back to normal. With the accelerator down to the floor and the revs still building the Renault surged to 120 miles per hour. He checked his mirror and the Volvo had responded. From then on he knew he had company.

Time for a change of plan, he slowed right down and stopped; then watched the Volvo driver's reaction. He also slowed but he didn't stop, instead he drove past at a more respectable speed, just about slow enough for Richard to get a glimpse of the driver's face which he felt looked familiar. He wasn't sure but he could have sworn that he looked remarkably like Danny, Fionnuala's brother, but he had passed by before he had chance to get a good look at him.

If it is Danny then why is he following me, is he under orders and if so does that mean they, the 'circus', know I'm here? This is not good news so you had better sit tight for a little while and see what happens.

After Paul's visit by the three musketeers, as they had christened them, and his own previous experience, life held few surprises anymore. Both he and Paul had contacted a number of people in their quest to find out who the three were and at one stage Richard even wondered if they were from his old unit, but further checks with a few army acquaintances had drawn a blank. The guy with the shattered arm would certainly have required specialist hospital attention, but discreet enquiries to various hospitals carried out by Sir James had even drawn a blank. It left only one option, and that was, they must have been from Ireland. This was a conundrum in itself because if they were from Ireland which faction were they from – O'Shea's Officials, the South Armagh lot or it may even be the same lot who took out the 'big man', his friend Sean O'Donald, there was just no way of telling. At this juncture Richard felt sure that whoever they were they must have come from Ireland. It never occurred to him that they may well have come from elsewhere! He waited for a few more minutes, just to make sure that his erstwhile shadow was not about to return, before setting off again at a more leisurely pace.

It wasn't long before Rosie's bungalow came into sight. He slowed down as he approached the entrance, checked and double checked his rear view mirror for any possible tail. Everything was as it should be – no vehicles in sight either to the front or the rear. Nothing had changed; it was exactly as he remembered even down to the sundial in the centre of the neatly mowed lawn. He drove slowly past and parked a little further on, gave a final check in both directions to make sure nothing looked out of place and got out of the car.

It didn't take long to cover the short distance to Rosie's front door and with heart pounding he gave the bell three short rings, three long rings and three short rings, the same coded signal he had used on his last visit, hopefully it hadn't changed.

He listened intently to hear any sounds of movement, but nothing. The idea that she may have moved crossed his mind.

Perhaps there is a new contact or maybe the department's old boy network has told Rosie about my troubles and that I'm no longer a member of the 'circus'.

These and many other thoughts flashed through his head as he waited on the doorstep. He was about to give up when he thought he saw one of the heavy net curtains move ever so slightly. He could have sworn he caught a glimpse of Rosie.

Inside the front room of the bungalow Rosie carefully eased back a corner of the curtain to check who it was who had given an out of date coded ring on her doorbell.

The last time that was used was way back; in fact it's so long ago I can't even remember the year. In fact it was the night Austen was picked up by Richard James codename Ferryman.

She could only see the caller's profile, from where she was she couldn't quite see his face and yet there was something recognizable about his stance. Briefly he turned towards the window before turning away again; she dropped the curtain and stepped back out of sight so he didn't see her. Even though she had only caught a glimpse of him there was something familiar about his face. Another check to make sure he was alone; after all she didn't want any nasty surprises when she opened the door. He was alone, but even so just as a safeguard, she pushed the Browning 9.00mm into the waistband round the back of her jeans and went to answer the door.

Richard was just about to leave when the door opened and Rosie, her face expressionless, was framed in the doorway. The same old Rosie, she hadn't changed much, perhaps the odd one or two laughter lines had appeared but otherwise she looked just the same.

"Hello Rosie."

She looked puzzled, at first she couldn't place him, then recognition dawned and her eyes twinkled and a broad grin crossed her face.

"Richard, it is you," he nodded. "Well what are you doing here? Come in, come in. Why didn't they tell me you were coming?" He stepped through the open door into the hallway. "What a surprise, it's good to see you," she said in a soft Irish lilt as she closed the front door. My you are looking grand; the world must be treating you well. Would you be having a drop o' tea then?" she enquired

"Yes please Rosie I'd love a cup of tea."

"Then you had best come into the kitchen and tell me what you've been up to since I last saw you." She ushered him into the kitchen, "sit yourself down then," she said indicating one of the pine kitchen chairs as she switched on the electric kettle. "It must be a few years now. So come on tell me how's things over the other side o' the water?"

"Haven't you heard?" Richard casually asked.

"Heard what?"

"Anything, anything at all?" The way she was towards him inferred she didn't know about his demise. *Could it all be an act?* The question he'd asked himself was immediately answered by her comment.

"Richard, at times I wonder if the department know I exist. They tell me nothing."

"Well officially it's always been like that Rosie, a need to know basis, but then there's always the bush telegraph."

"Richard honestly whether official or unofficial I have heard nothing."

"Hmm" Richard studied her face as he asked, "what's going on Rosie?"

"How do you mean?" she asked with a puzzled look on her face. Richard was silent. He stared hard at Rosie wondering how much to tell her. "Rosie, do you still work through the

Ambassador's office in Dublin, or are you handled through the Irish desk in London?"

"Dublin. Nothing's changed. Why?"

Her answer made things a little easier as he knew that there was a good chance she had not been tainted. "Just curious that's all," he answered. "Tell me, how well do you know Wyman?" She shrugged her shoulders.

"Not too well, wasn't he Austen's handler?" she asked.

"Yes he was." Richard answered then fell silent.

"What's this all about Richard?"

"Just a few more questions Rosie and then I'll tell you what I can. Do you have any contact with him?"

"No" came the reply.

"So who does he handle now over here?" Rosie was beginning to sense that there was something she was missing here. Why was he asking all these questions she wondered, especially as he worked for HQ, he should know the answers unless…

"Please answer the question Rosie, who does he handle now?"

"Excuse me Richard," she said as she made to get up.

"Sit down Rosie." Richard's tone was different. His voice was hard and business like. Her reaction was quick; her hand reached for the Browning, but his had been quicker. His eyes never moved from her face as she saw the Browning appear in his hands. She sat down. "Sorry it has to be this way Rosie. Now please answer my question, who does Wyman handle now?"

"It's a guy in C3 Gardai Special Branch in Dublin."

"Is his name Danny?" Richard asked.

"Yes I think so."

"Oh dear, that's not so good."

"Why, what's this all about?" He thought long and hard about the answers she had given and decided that she was telling the truth when she'd said she hadn't heard anything. He also had a strange feeling that his being tailed by Danny could have certain repercussions not only for him but perhaps for Rosie, so she deserved to know. Anyway he needed to start building his private network sooner rather than later.

"Listen Rosie," his voice was softer now, "what I'm about to tell you is to be treated as TOP SECRET and I need your reassurance that whatever happens you will not divulge a word to anyone, including Dublin or London. Do I have your word on this?" She nodded. Richard pursed his lips. "OK now slowly, ever so slowly get up and move over here." She got up and walked over to Richard. "Now turn round so I can see your back." With a deft movement he had hooked her Browning out of her waistband and it clattered to the floor. "Right now go and sit back down where you were." She did as she was told. As soon as she was seated Richard retrieved her weapon and placed it with his on the table in front of him. He then proceeded to tell her a little about his latest operation and how he needed to set up a net to catch a suspected 'mole' within the 'circus', beginning with the operation known as *Damocles* and moving on to the failed attempt to snatch 'slab' Riley. He told her how someone somewhere had provided bad intelligence about the back-up generators which had ultimately cost operators' lives. How with Wyman's help he had got Jock out and how he and Wyman were attacked in the safe house. He told her everything.

"So do you think Wyman's the mole?" she asked.

"I'm not sure, but one thing I'm certain of, is that whenever he has been involved things have had a habit of going tits up."

"But he helped you get Jock out didn't he?"

"Yes I know, but I've done a couple of jobs with him now and on each occasion things went wrong. Look at what happened to Austen, Wyman was his handler, Austen gets arrested, the British Government denounce him and he ends up in prison. It just seems that there are a lot of coincidences that are difficult to explain."

"So how can I help?"

"See what else you can find out about Wyman. Where does he really fit in? Apart from Danny does he handle anybody else in the Dublin sector? Has he been involved with any other failed operations apart from the ones I've told you about? In fact anything that you feel will help." Richard glanced at his watch; it was time to make a move. "Here Rosie," he passed her the Browning back, "I must go so you take care and look after yourself," he said as he stood up to leave. "See what you can find out for me and I'll be in touch next week, and just for the record from here on I shall be referred to as *'Beggarman'.*"

"Huh, *Beggarman* you say, so who are the other characters?"

"Other characters, what do you mean by other characters?"

"Well, *Rich-man, Poor-man, Beggarman, Thief* of course!" She said with a wry smile.

"Ah yes of course." Richard smiled, "let's just say that because of what the 'mole' is and what they, whoever they are, stand for, I have given him or her the name *Thief.*"

It was late afternoon when Wyman received the telephone call.

"Danny here. Richard James arrived Dublin early morning ferry."

"So why haven't you called until now Danny?"

"Too many eyes and ears."

"OK. So where is he now?"

"I followed him to outskirts of Swords but he spotted me and stopped, so I passed him and carried on up the road so as not to raise his suspicions any more than necessary."

"Why is he here?" asked Wyman. Before Danny could answer Wyman's question his office door opened and Ryan, one of Danny's colleagues, entered. "Sorry wrong number," he said and replaced the phone. "Damn, I must have dialled it wrong," he muttered as if to himself but loud enough for Ryan to hear.

"What's the matter Danny?" his colleague asked.

"Oh, sorry didn't realise you were there Ryan," Danny glibly said hoping that Ryan hadn't noticed anything. "What did you say?"

"I wondered what you were talking about that's all."

"Nothing really, I was just muttering to myself. Actually I was trying to phone my sister Fionnuala but got a wrong number. I was sure I dialled it right but…"

"To be sure you did Danny. Since they went over to this new exchange, it's always happening."

At five on the dot Richard left Rosie and made his way back to his car. He had just closed the door and started the engine as a motorcycle travelling at speed came along the road towards him. As it approached where he was parked the engine note changed as the driver changed down the gears and braked viciously. Richard turned and watched in horror as the motorcycle drew level with Rosie's place. Too late he realised, there was a flash of flame as a rocket propelled grenade was launched by the pillion directly at Rosie's front door and where she was standing. In the same instant as he saw the flash he heard a deafening explosion and a ball of fire engulfed the front door. Where the door had been was now nothing more than a gaping hole with flames licking up towards the sky and the motorcycle a mere speck in the distance.

"No, no. Rosieeee." Richard slung open the car door and ran back to the bungalow, but he knew there was nothing he could do. What had once been a neat and tidy garden was now like a builder's yard covered in chards of glass and rubble. It was obvious to Richard that somebody somewhere didn't want Rosie talking to him.

Faintly at first he could hear the wail of the Gardai and Emergency sirens and as the seconds ticked by the wailing grew louder and louder until they sounded as if they were seconds away. There was nothing here for him now and he knew he had to get away as quickly as possible. He ran back to the car, slammed the door and floored the accelerator. In seconds he came to a junction, braked hard, made sure there was nothing coming and did a u-turn then with vicious acceleration he headed back towards Dublin and the motorway.

It didn't take him long to get to the motorway and head north for Belfast and once there he would telephone Jean O'Donald the widow of Sean, his late friend and handler, and hopefully she would put him up. His plan was to meet up with Jean to try and enlist her help; also he hoped she could arrange a meeting with Jimmy with whom he had worked in the 'circus' before being sold down the river by Her Majesty's Government (HMG). That was his plan, but things can change in this line of work so it pays to be adaptable. As the sign for Drogheda and Dundalk loomed up ahead a thought occurred to him.

A visit to Eamonn may well be fruitful.

Eamonn was a double agent working for British Intelligence but was also a senior member of the Official IRA. Richard knew that Eamonn would co-operate with him, if only to avoid his cover being blown to Breandán O'Shea. It then occurred to him, that whilst he was in the area he might as well look up Seamus too, so killing two birds with one stone. Although they both reported to Lisburn and may well be aware of his demise in the 'circus' he felt it was well worth the minimal risk involved.

As he took the slip road off the motorway, his thoughts went back to that fateful moment outside Rosie's bungalow when the pillion on the motorbike launched the rocket propelled grenade. He thought about Danny.

How did he know I was coming to Ireland there?

There was only one person who knew of his plan and that was Paul. He immediately pushed the thought out of his mind, mad with himself for even considering such an ill conceived idea. But no matter how hard he tried, the idea it was linked to Paul kept resurfacing time and time again. Perhaps Paul had inadvertently said something to someone and from this the department had got to know and decided to act. It had been a slick operation.

His mind wandered back to the eighties when he had driven the Cortina, laden with explosives and a timer, into the centre of Dublin to make it look like a terrorist car bomb attack. This attack had certain similarities; the idea of using a motorcyclist to make it look like an IRA attack had all the hallmarks of a 'hit' by the department which, luckily for him, had gone wrong. He thought that by missing him they had botched it and missed their main target. But then something didn't quite gel. Had he been the real target the department would have had him under surveillance from the very start. They would have used a team of tails to keep tabs on him. They would know his every move. They would have followed him to the Ferry Terminal and would have set up observation teams on all his known contacts including Rosie. They would have tailed him upon arrival; sure they had done that but he had spotted Danny. There again, if he was the target, then why wasn't he taken out before? If they had wanted it to look like an IRA attack they could have taken him out whilst he was at Rosie's. No, he wasn't the target and more to the point it wasn't the department who carried out the *hit* because there were far too many flaws.

The appearance of Danny was coincidental, so if it wasn't the department who was it? The more he thought about it the greater the enigma. He was like a dog with a bone; he kept tossing the same questions about in his head hoping that he would spot the missing link. He went over his conversation with Rosie time and time again. Where or who was the common denominator? What had Rosie and Danny in common? Danny was Irish and Rosie was Irish, they both worked in the twenty-six counties and for the British Secret Service so they both had handlers. He slammed the brakes on and the car skidded to a halt.

"Christ Richard", he said out loud, "I think you've got it." He thought it through again carefully. They both had handlers, what had Rosie said about her handler? No matter how much he tried he didn't recollect her saying anything about her handler apart from she still worked through Dublin. The fact of the matter was that he was the one doing most of the talking. He had been talking about Wyman... Danny, yes Danny his handler was Wyman. Austen's handler was Wyman; my back-up had been Wyman. The safe house in Ulster was one of Wyman's and Carl was Wyman's driver. Wyman and Danny were both responsible for the data gathered on Operation Orpheus, and that went tits up. So Danny picks me up at the docks, he tails me to the outskirts of Swords. I stop, he passes me but does not return nor do I see him en route. As a field operator he was obviously alerted to my arrival, but by whom, or was it just by chance? Having picked me up and tailed me, then passed me, he would have to advise his handler so he contacts Wyman. But Wyman has no connections with paramilitary groups, or if he has he has kept that very quiet.

Hmm, it appears as if Wyman is connected but how?

He thought a little more about this aspect but still couldn't find the answer. There was something else bothering him and that was if Wyman was the man then how was he involved with Paul and his arrest? No it just didn't stack up. In the end he pushed the conundrum to the back of his mind and once again continued on his way.

It wasn't long before he was passing the lane to the Tara Hotel which held a veritable treasure trove of memories some fond and some not so fond. On the left, just a stone's throw from the approach to the Tara, was a track leading to the farm where Seamus lived and on an impulse Richard decided to see if he was at home. Seamus, although not the man's real name but a codename, was a brilliant explosives expert who had served in the Royal Navy as a frogman saboteur and then went on to be an instructor at Gosport and Hereford. The last time Richard had seen Seamus was back in the eighties when, by using his knowledge of explosives, they carried out successfully the first stage of Operation Orpheus.

Richard turned the car into the lane and bumped and jolted his way towards the farm where he would renew his acquaintance with Seamus in the hope that he could help him in his quest to uncover the 'mole'. Arriving at the gate it was obvious to him that the place was deserted and judging by the height of the weeds it had been deserted for quite some time. He opened the gate and swung the Renault into the drive where he parked. He decided that as he was here it would not hurt to take a look around and there just may be a clue as to where the man had gone. He grasped the door handle and turned it. To his immense surprise the door opened. Pushing it wider Richard let himself in and proceeded to take a look around. His first port of call was the kitchen cum living room where he found, to his surprise, the old kitchen table and chairs. In the drawers he found cutlery and the cupboards still housed plates, mugs and cooking utensils, but very little else. Every where he looked he drew a blank. It was in the very last drawer. A drawer that held nothing, he was just about to push it closed with disgust when he caught sight of what appeared to be a torn piece of paper jammed into a split in the wood. Carefully he removed the drawer from its runners and teased the piece of paper out from the split which upon closer examination revealed the name Lamar. The letters jumped off the paper at Richard causing his heart to skip a beat and a surge of adrenalin pumped through his body. The last time he had come across this name was back in the eighties before he had been 'hospitalised', so what was the connection between Seamus and Lamar, how did Seamus fit into all of this? If he could find Seamus then he could ask him, but as to where he had gone that was anyone's guess.

Upstairs the bedrooms were still fully furnished but all the signs were that the place had not been lived in for some time. In the first bedroom he carefully and systematically went through all the drawers searching for any clues as to the whereabouts of the owner, but nothing. He got down on his hands and knees and slowly on all fours he moved along the skirting board, inspecting the carpet, closely examining the edge. He was looking for tell-tale signs of lifting which would indicate that at some time or other the carpet had been lifted away and rolled back – but nothing. He repeated the painstaking process in the second bedroom with the same result. Then finally he entered the third small bedroom. Again the same result and he was about to give up on the idea, when he felt rather than heard the squeak from the loose floorboard beneath his step as he walked from the room. He immediately dropped on all fours again only this time pressing all around him until he felt the slight movement of the loose floorboard.

Upon closer examination of the carpet he could just discern a slight ruck where the fitted carpet at some time had been disturbed. His intuition told him he had found what he was looking for. After twenty minutes of tedious use with his penknife his painstaking effort paid off and he rolled back the carpet to reveal a floorboard that had been carefully sawn and screwed back in place. Using the blade of his knife as a screwdriver he released the piece of floorboard to expose a void beneath the floor – there was nothing to be seen, it was empty. Just to make certain that it was empty and that Seamus had removed everything Richard laid flat out in the prone position and reached in as far as he could. With arm outstretched and in this position he swept his hand around beneath the floorboards. Suddenly his finger brushed against something. It felt like a note book or something.

If only – ah yes.

He managed to flick it a little way toward the opening.

Another flick and I'll be able to get it.

He withdrew a cheap notebook, the pages held together with a spiralled wire binder. Some of the pages had been removed and all that was left was a few blank sheets. For the moment he put the notebook aside and did a final check of the void before screwing the floorboard back into place. He carefully rolled back the carpet and pushed the edge back under the skirting. Picking up the notebook Richard gave one last look around to make sure that he had left everything as it was before he had lifted the carpet. A further check that there were no tell-tale signs of his visit and that the carpet had been replaced and he made his way back downstairs.

Back downstairs in the kitchen Richard considered his next move. Once more he studied the torn piece of paper with the name Lamar written on it.

Damn it Seamus I trusted you so where do you stand in all this?

In the depth of his memory he recollected something he had been taught whilst training at Fort Monkton.

Graphite powder. 'Remember gentlemen tip the graphite powder onto the sheet and gently spread it over the sheet without touching it, otherwise it will smudge the image'.

All he needed was some graphite powder. When he was operational he always used to carry some in a tin in his car, but it was years since he had used it and the tin had long since gone. Then it occurred to him – Rosie's place.

Yes, that's it. Of course she would have some. It was standard issue.

With that thought he left the farm pulling the door closed as he departed.

Darkness was closing in as Richard drove slowly past Rosie's bungalow and he was surprised to see how much of it was untouched. It seemed as if the resultant damage from the attack was minimal and had only taken out the front door and the front windows. The main body of the property plus the garage remained intact. The Gardai appeared to have been and gone although their blue tape was still across the front gate and drive showing that they still had it sealed off and were treating it as a crime scene, but there was no sign of any ongoing investigation.

After a second slow drive past he decided to park his car in the same place as he had done earlier that day and retrieving a torch from his glove box he made his way back to Rosie's. Having made a final check just to confirm that there was nobody around he quickly ducked beneath the tape and headed for the blackened aperture that had previously been the front porch and door. He carefully picked his way over rubble and fallen masonry into the blackness beyond, pausing briefly to listen for any sounds that may indicate that someone else was there. Silence, it hit as an eerie heavy silence. He could taste the acrid taste of dust and cordite, the smell of smoke still heavy in the air.

Shrouded in the darkness of what was once a tastefully decorated hallway, but was now nothing more than a burnt out shell, and with a hand over the lens he switched on his torch, his fingers causing the light to disperse and fragment in such a way as to reduce the risk of his presence being spotted by someone passing by. It didn't take him long to make his way into the main body of the property and subsequently into the kitchen. He remembered Rosie once showing him where she kept her communication system secreted, but he wouldn't mind betting that the Gardai had already thoroughly searched the premises. If they had found her system and logs etc then they would know that she had been working for a foreign Government, that is of course if they didn't already know previously and fed her name to the IRA.

Now where is that panel, that's if the plods haven't found it?

Richard was now happy to scan around with the full beam of his torch and was both surprised and pleased to see the kitchen virtually intact. He slowly scanned the scene with his torch until the light picked out the Aga cooker. He shone the torch on the Aga's chimney and traced it upwards with the shaft of light. It seemed intact. He moved quickly over to the Aga and running his hand along the cold metal of its chimney he felt for the two concealed clips that held the chimney in place, Voila. Richard undid the two clips and removed the chimney section immediately exposing a demountable panel that he could see by the light of his torch had not been disturbed.

In under thirty seconds he had recovered log books, small transceiver, a Browning 9.00mm, code books and a small tin of graphite powder. He had obtained what he had come for and more besides. Carefully he replaced the panel, re-connected the chimney and slowly made his way back the way he had come.

Richard's Renault 21 bumped and jarred along the lane leading to the farm that Seamus had once inhabited. Having left Rosie's he had decided to use the farm as a base, after all it was off the main road and he felt secure in the knowledge that he could stay there undiscovered for a few days if necessary, but for all that he didn't intend to outstay his welcome. His intention was to have something to eat, check out the log books he had retrieved from Rosie's and try and get some sort of lead on Seamus. He had considered the possibility of Seamus returning to the farm unannounced, but felt that was unlikely and it was a risk he was prepared to take, after all he had come to the farm with the intention of seeing the man in the first place. What is more he drew comfort from the knowledge that he was armed. His plan was to check if the electric was still connected, get a fire going, have something to eat and the provided there was light, to work on the information he had. Failing that he would eat, and work on the information at first light. He swung the car round the back of the farmhouse so it was not readily visible to any would-be visitors. Taking his torch he picked his way through the grass and weeds to the front door and started his hunt for the electricity supply. It didn't take long to find and mercifully it was still connected. At least he had light and power. The next thing to do was to get the fire going and have something to eat.

Richard spread a sheet of newspaper out on the table in front of him and lay the blank page from the notebook on the sheet. Carefully, very carefully, he poured some graphite powder onto the sheet in front of him. Then with steady hands he picked up the sheet and very slowly tilted one way then the next, letting the black graphite powder run all over the page covering every last vestige of white paper. Then he tipped the messy black powder onto the newspaper. He could quite clearly see the lines linking the faint outline of names. Richard copied out exactly what he saw. It appeared to be some sort of Social Network Diagram linking various individuals. On the diagram appeared the names Austen, Wyman, Eamonn and Danny all of which linked to MI6. These four names were linked directly, but that wasn't all. The name Lamar was also on the diagram as a central figure, yet not linked directly to anyone in particular but to the IRSP and the IRA with a further link from him to a question mark in a box stating UK. From MI6 there was a dotted line via the question mark UK.

Why had that link been drawn, what did Seamus know?

The dotted line showed that Seamus had linked MI6 indirectly with Lamar and subsequently the IRA. In a way it also confirmed that Wyman was nothing to do with the leaks and that they were coming from a higher authority. The mole was very deep inside the heart of the intelligence network! Richard pondered over what he now saw.

However there was something wrong, if this were the case then how come I was followed by Danny and shortly afterwards Rosie was killed?

He knew Eamonn was a double agent and he was linked to Danny and Wyman, but if he was the link to the leaks it would leave too much unexplained. No there was something he was missing.

He studied the information until his mind glazed over and the sheet of newsprint raced up at him, and the graphite powder spread across his face. He slept like this, on the table, the graphite smeared across his cheeks.

Chapter 6

The sun streamed in through the kitchen window.

The whistle blew shrilly as the sun streamed in through the carriage window. The carriage rocked to and fro as the whistle got louder. The Ticket Inspector knew his name.

Suddenly he was awake. The aroma of freshly made coffee tickled his nostrils. Where was he? His eyes slowly focussed on the steaming mug of drink and he lifted his head.

Shit!

He was looking across the kitchen and framed in the door was Seamus.

"Good morning Richard, and what are you doing here?" Levelled at his head was a Browning 9.00mm.

Shit Richard now you're in trouble.

"Hello Seamus. I arrived last night. I came to see you…"

"I can see that, and I notice you've been digging about…found my old notepad and used the old graphite powder. Well Richard what are you doing here?" he asked quite menacingly.

"As I said Seamus, I came to see you. Found the place all shut up. The signs were it hadn't been lived in for some time so I tried to find some clues to your whereabouts…that's all." Seamus studied Richard's face. He wasn't sure whether to believe him or not.

Come on Seamus don't piss me about.

"You'd better drink your coffee before it gets cold."

Richard picked up the mug of steaming coffee and sipped it whilst he tried to work out whose side Seamus was really on. They both sat in silence, Richard drinking his coffee and Seamus studying Richard, wondering what he should do about this interloper. Seamus broke the silence.

"I heard you were out of the 'circus'."

"Did you?"

"Yeah, something to do with a breakdown…is that right?"

What else have you been told Seamus?

"No that's not quite right, but tell me what's been said about my having a breakdown, what has everyone been told?" Seamus fell silent. He thought about it for a while.

There had been a rumour that someone somewhere wanted Richard out. There was also a rumour about there being a mole in the 'circus' so was he the mole? Is that why he had a so called breakdown?'

"Some say that you had a rough time of it, and you got stitched up, but others say you had a breakdown," he paused to take a mouthful of steaming coffee then continued. "By the way it has been rumoured that there is a mole in the 'circus', have you heard that one?" He studied Richard's face whilst he drank his coffee, but Richard didn't flinch, nor did he reply straight away. Instead he stared steadfastly back at Seamus for a time.

Can you be trusted Seamus? The question had no sooner popped into his head before it was gone. *Damn it, I need to trust someone. I need help.*

"OK Seamus I'll tell you what happened. After our little jolly when we set up the bombing in Dublin, I was eventually given an operation called Operation Orpheus. I won't bore you with the details, but the bottom line was that we were to snatch a bloke called 'slab' Riley, right here in the twenty-six counties, but the operation failed. We took losses, heavy losses, some badly wounded and others killed, but I managed to get out and the failure was put down to bad intelligence. Later we had another series of problems and I was ultimately removed from the 'circus' and placed in a psychiatric unit with a supposed nervous breakdown, but that was a cover-up. The truth is, that for some inexplicable reason, I was actually drugged and removed from my home and it's because of these events that I am here. I needed to speak to you to see if you could help throw some light on things." Richard looked up at Seamus, "Seamus I need your help. Will you help me?" Seamus thought long and hard about what Richard had said. He needed to take his time on this.

If what he says is true then perhaps we can work together on finding this mole, but first of all I have to do some checks. The first person to talk to is Eamonn who will check it out with Wyman.

Deep down his gut feeling was to help Richard, his intuition was also to help him, but his training told him to be suspicious and not to trust him.

"OK Richard on one condition." Seamus had made his decision.

"And that is what?"

"I need to check a few things with my contacts first. So in the meantime I'm afraid I'll need to…" Seamus moved in closer to Richard and suddenly swung the butt of his Browning against Richard's skull. "Sorry chum…" he muttered as Richard's body slumped forward, his head crashing on to the table and into the graphite powder once again. Seamus bundled the now limp form of Richard on to the floor. He then opened one of the cupboards and took out some wide duck tape, an old scarf and some chord with which he quickly and expertly tied Richard's arms behind his back and his legs together. He then ran a length of cord from his legs to the one that tied his arms pulling it tight, forcing the soles of Richard's shoes hard up against his buttocks. With a length of duck tape across Richard's mouth and the scarf blindfolding him Seamus felt happy that he could now leave, secure in the knowledge that Mr James was going nowhere. The only thing he now needed to do was to contact control and advise them of this latest complication.

Slowly the deep blackness receded only to be replaced by a lighter darkness. Richard gave an involuntary moan at the excruciating pain in his head.

Where am I?

Through the pounding headache, the fuzziness and the fog in his brain slowly started to clear. Gradually it all came back to him. How he had returned to the old farm and searched it. How he found the scrap of paper with the name Lamar scribbled on it and the old notebook with the Social Network Diagram showing all the links. Then he must have fallen asleep because the next thing he remembered was Seamus standing there. He remembered thinking he needed help.

Huh! What was that my old son, could you trust Seamus? Well I think you have your answer.

He tried to move but that only made the throbbing in his head worse and caused him to feel nauseous. He wondered how long he had been unconscious and when Seamus would return?

Shit! Now what are you going to do Richard?

Once more he tried to manoeuvre himself into a more comfortable position and again the dull throb in his head increased to a pounding and no matter what he tried he wasn't going anywhere.

He must have blacked out again because he hadn't heard the door or any movement, but suddenly the rope pulling his feet up towards his buttocks went slack and he could move his legs. He felt someone pulling at him. He realised that they were trying to sit him up.

Sit up Richard. Come on help yourself.

He managed, with the other person's help, to manoeuvre himself into a seated position. A faint yet subtle smell, which he was sure he recognised, invaded his nostrils. Whoever the person was he was sure it was a woman. This was confirmed as he felt long hair momentarily brush against his cheek and he could now smell her perfume.

Who is she?

Next he felt a sawing at his wrists then the pressure of his bonds was released and his hands were free. With fingers slightly shaking he pulled and tugged at the knotted scarf about his head that served to blindfold him, hoping to see who his benefactor was. But too late, he heard the door close just as the knot loosened. Richard tore the scarf away from his eyes, hoping to at least catch a glimpse of her through the window, but the sound of a car's engine confirmed that he had missed his opportunity.

The car bucked and the steering wheel jumped and spun as the slender fingers of the driver gripped tightly to the wheel. She hurriedly brushed the long brown hair from her face as she fought with the steering wheel as the car sped along the rutted track leading to the road. She managed a quick glance in the rear view mirror confirming that Richard James was still inside the boarded up farmhouse and managed a faint smile.

If only you knew the half of it Richard James, if only...

With that thought still in her mind she reached the main Dublin road and turned right towards Dublin. At last she could afford to relax a little and let her mind drift back to earlier times.

How did that Beatles song go...?

She glanced up at the mirror, smiled and started to hum the melody of 'I wanna hold your hand'.

Yes Richard James I did hold your hand all right and you certainly were very close to me that sunny afternoon when you called in for coffee. We made love in the lounge as Dean Martin crooned his way through 'Gentle on my mind'. I teased you about not remembering me in my nurse's uniform when I came with Brother O'Leary from the Order to collect Noel and take him back to the clinic. We kissed and you were so sorry about knocking the coffee over with your foot. Ah yes Richard things could have been so very different had you known who I really worked for, but there again at that time you probably had never heard of Sir James Johnstone let alone knew that I actually worked for him. The last instruction from Sir James was that I was to stay in the shadows and not to compromise my position – ah what a pity.

She swung the car into a narrow tree lined country lane which according to the sign announced it was a Private Drive with access to O'Shea Fruit Farm and the Tara Hotel. After three or four hundred yards the road gently swung to the left through an open gateway with a sign welcoming patrons to the Tara Hotel. A narrower lane peeled off to the right and it was along this lane the young lady went. She continued along here eventually rounding a tight bend whereupon a cottage with its own parking area came into view. It was here that the young lady stopped and still humming to herself she parked her car and went into the cottage.

Richard hurriedly grabbed hold of the notebook and scrabbled around on the table for something to write with. Although he had not seen who had released him he had managed to get the car's registration number as it drove off up the cart track. He knew from the faint smell of perfume that it was a girl. His heart missed a beat.

Could it be his old love Fionnuala, but if it was why hadn't she waited?

He needed to trace the vehicle, because that vehicle carried the person he could trust.

The Renault 21 bumped along the deeply rutted lane as Richard headed away from the farmhouse towards the main road. Armed with the old notebook with the registration number, the piece of paper with Lamar scribbled on it and the tin of graphite, Richard decided to set about tracing the whereabouts of his mystery lady. In his mind there were two possibilities, one was the beautiful Fionnuala and the other was Jean O'Donald.

Ah yes Fionnuala my colleen, the beautiful Fionnuala with her long hair and that gentle Irish lilt. Ah yes…If anyone could be trusted she could. After all we had been more than good friends for quite some time, if only I knew where to find her.

Jean O'Donald was the widow of Sean, his old friend and colleague from his days in the 'circus'. He had been killed by a car bomb. After his death Jean had looked to Richard for support in her hour of need and through the troubled days and months that followed they became great friends, so she could equally have been the one to set him free, but the same question arose.

If it was Jean why had she been in such a hurry to leave? It doesn't make sense!

Even as he thought about his next move the main road loomed ahead. Here he paused and considered his options.

Right towards Dublin, or left towards the border and Lisburn?

He remembered. Fionnuala had once said she lived in a small place called Corke Abbey near Dublin so on a hunch he turned right. In the distance he could just make out the lane on the left to the Tara Hotel and on an impulse he changed his mind. As he approached the tree lined lane he slowed the Renault and indicated to turn down the lane to the hotel. Perhaps Noel still worked there as the night porter he thought to himself.

If anyone can tell me where I can find Fionnuala it's Noel.

With that thought uppermost in his mind Richard drove in through the imposing gateway and parked in the car park. He paused before opening the door, taking a few minutes to look around his surroundings just to get his bearings. Nothing had changed. Still the same old Tara, it was like coming home.

It was dark by the time Richard left the Tara and once more headed down the lane to the main Dublin road. His plan to trace Fionnuala had not quite worked as he had expected. Yes he had seen Noel, but only briefly. Unfortunately Noel had lost track of the beautiful Fionnuala, but that wasn't to say he couldn't track her down he just needed a little time, but unfortunately that was a rare commodity for the present and something that Richard had little of. As he approached the main road Richard pushed all thoughts of his beloved Fionnuala firmly out of his head and turned right heading north toward the border and eventually Lisburn where Jean O'Donald lived, but things could well have turned out differently had Richard realised how close he had been to unearthing his rescuer's true identity.

Chapter 7

It was already getting dark outside as Eleanor pulled the curtains closed and switched on the small table lamp. She gave an involuntary shiver and decided she would light the fire. The evenings were now drawing in and autumn was getting ever closer. The trees in the lane sensed that winter was on its way and there was a subtle change in the colour of the leaves as they prepared for the long cold nights ahead. It wasn't long before the fire threw out its warmth and the flames cast long flickering shadows on the sitting room wall; the room was snug and inviting just as it had been that fateful day when Richard James had arrived for coffee.

Ah yes indeed. That was an afternoon to remember with the sunlight streaming through the windows as we made love. Interesting how things turn out, how he eventually became involved with my great friend Fionnuala.

She glanced at her watch.

Is that the time? She'll be home now.

Eleanor reached for the telephone and dialled a Dublin number and waited. A girl's voice answered.

"Hello Fionnuala. It's Eleanor. Yes I found him and he was fine, a little tied up at the time but he's now free. No I'm sure he doesn't know and that's probably just as well…of course I'll let you know just as soon as I know…Yes, I spoke to Noel at the Tara, and yes he said he would help us…Of course…Will you let London know? OK, I'll leave it with you then…so you'll…I see. OK bye, speak to you soon."

OK Mr James, so what are you going to do now? Head for Jean O'Donald's I hope.

Richard, feeling slightly apprehensive about Jean O'Donald's reaction at seeing him after all this time, drove along the now familiar road towards her house. The last time they had met was some three or four years ago after her husband was viciously murdered by a car bomb attack and at the time she was feeling very vulnerable. Even though Jean was an old friend, circumstances and recent events may well have changed everything, depending on what she had been told about his so-called *breakdown.*

As Richard swung the Renault in through the open gates of Jean's driveway and drove up toward the house the whole area was immediately bathed in light. As an additional security measure passive infrared detectors had been installed along the drive since his last visit, which would automatically trigger the outside floodlights. In front of the garage stood a gleaming brand new BMW and it was alongside this he parked.

Hmm, not bad, he thought. *Obviously business is good!*

He sat in the Renault for a moment to gather his thoughts and to steady his breathing before getting out. Then, feeling slightly nervous he made his way to the front door.

Well here goes.

He reached up and pressed the doorbell and waited.

Perhaps she's not in. Rubbish her car's here.

As soon as he had come to that conclusion the door opened and there was Jean.

Too late to go now my old son.

"Hello Richard, what a nice surprise. Come in, come in."

Still the same old Jean.

"Sorry to drop in on you like this out of the blue so to speak," he said a little nervously, "but to be honest I need some help and you were…"

"Well come in," she said once more with enthusiasm cutting him off in mid sentence. She grabbed his hand and pulled him into the house. "Good to see you Richard and how on earth are you?" she asked and kissed him on the cheek. Immediately she made him feel welcome and any anxiety he may have been experiencing evaporated. "Here let me have your coat, and go on through to the lounge." Before he realised it he had forgotten all about his earlier apprehension, handed her his coat and was heading towards the lounge. Nothing had changed; the lounge was exactly as he remembered it to be.

Still as neat and tidy as it always was.

He paused in the doorway and looked about the room, picking up on all the finer details. The desk was still in the same place, the suite was the same. The room still had that warm homely feel about it.

"Go in Richard and sit down." He hadn't heard Jean's approach and gave an involuntary jump. "Sorry Richard, you seem a little on edge, still I'm sure a nice cup of tea will soon sort that out, or would you prefer something stronger?"

Damn it Jean after my recent trouble with Seamus I've good cause to be nervous!

"No I'm not on edge," he lied and gave a weak smile. "It's just that I was thinking how nice it was to be back here and I was daydreaming and didn't hear you coming, that's all," he finished off rather lamely. "I noticed you've got a new car, a BMW isn't it?" he asked changing the subject as he made his way over to one of the easy chairs and sat down.

"Oh let me see I bought it five or six weeks ago. What do you think?"

"Nice car. Do you like it?"

"Yes it's my type of car, comfortable, roomy and has the power if you need it. What would you like to drink, tea or something stronger?" She smiled wickedly.

"Oh…tea will be fine thanks."

"Tea it is then," she said as she made her way out through the open door to the kitchen only to return a few minutes later with a tray and a selection of biscuits which she placed on the low coffee table positioned between the two easy chairs.

"Help yourself to biscuits," she said as she picked up the jug of milk. "Milk and sugar?"

"Milk but no sugar thank you."

"Have you eaten?" she enquired.

"No, but don't worry."

"I can fix you a sandwich, or something a little more substantial if you like."

"No don't worry."

"It's no trouble Richard."

"No, honestly it's all right I'll get something later."

"If you're sure. Anyway where are you staying tonight?" she asked as she passed him the cup of tea.

Hopefully here.

"To be honest I haven't booked anywhere as I was intending to go back to Dublin…"

"Nonsense," she said interrupting him and flashing one of her disarming smiles. "You'll stay here and I will not take no as an answer."

"Well…seeing that you insist, I really appreciate it Jean."

Of course you'll stay especially after I heard about your little escapade with Seamus. Yes Richard love, it's a good job Fionnuala was tipped off by her brother and Eleanor was in the cottage otherwise you could have had a problem.

"That's settled then, the guest's room is already prepared." As soon as she said it she realised what she had said and could have kicked herself. Richard's look confirmed the fact that he suspected that she knew something.

Damn. You don't miss a trick Richard James.

"So were you expecting me?" he asked.

"No…no of course not," she answered trying hard to sound convincing. "I always have the bed made up as a matter of course. In fact you of all people should know that especially in this game, after all you never quite know when it might be needed," she said and smiled at him hoping that her hastily added explanation would cover her earlier faux pas. Richard looked at her for a moment or two as if he wasn't sure, but in the end he smiled.

That was a close call Jean O'Donald you need to be more careful in future.

"So what brings you here Richard?" Jean settled back into her armchair expectantly and waited for Richard to tell her the full story about what had happened to him since their last meeting some years previously, how both he and Paul had suffered the ignominy of being arrested, then the failed operation and how he was eventually removed to a psychiatric institution under the guise of having a breakdown.

"Well, that's the official line as put out by the 'circus', good old Richard James has retired on medical grounds, because of a breakdown."

"Well, did you?" asked Jean.

"Of course not," he replied angrily. "It was a total fabrication put out by the department." He then fell into a sullen silence. Jean considered what he had said for a few minutes before saying anything, then picking her words carefully she asked him why he hadn't suspected anything.

"You say that you were sitting at home when these individuals arrived and told you they were from Ministry." He nodded and she continued. "Surely you smelled a rat?"

"No not really," he replied. "You see when they said they were from the Ministry, I assumed they meant the Ministry of Agriculture and Fisheries after all we ran a farm, so it was quite feasible, besides what would you think?" Jean thought about it for a moment or two and in the end had to agree that it did seem quite feasible.

"So tell me Richard, who do you think is behind it, who do you think stitched you up?" He looked at Jean and shrugged his shoulders.

"I don't know, but there is one thing for sure…"

"And that is?"

"That you are the only person I can trust with this information." Richard took a deep breath before continuing. "Look at what's happened up until now. Sean is murdered…" he paused and stuck up his thumb. "Number two; I'm setup with bad intelligence on a raid…" once again he paused sticking up a finger. "Number three; we return to a safe house but are ambushed…" another pause and he sticks up a second finger. "Number four, Paul and I are arrested…" he sticks up a third finger and pauses once more. "Number five, six and seven, I am drugged, sectioned and shot at…" Richard raises a further thumb and two fingers on his other hand. "I am no longer part of the 'circus' that is number nine. In fact I think it was you yourself who warned me about some person or persons in high places who was out to get me. If I now add the break-in at my solicitor's office and the recent attack on Paul that makes number ten and eleven inexplicable incidents in all and there are others. The list gets longer and longer," again he could feel the anger beginning to bubble up inside him. "Do I need to go on Jean?"

"No Richard I take your point."

"So will you help me trap this 'mole'?" he asked her in a quiet voice and waited for her to answer. Jean sat in silence as she mulled over what Richard had said. She poked it and prodded it, but was still not sure of how she could really help him.

"Look Richard," she said after a short while, "I would love to help but as to how well…" she left the rest hanging. "Let me get you something to eat," she said changing the subject, "come on Richard; come through to the kitchen whilst I prepare you a meal."

It wasn't too long before Richard was sitting at the table tucking in to a large grilled rump steak garnished with mushrooms and salad, but Jean was still unsure as to how she could help, when suddenly she remembered something that Sean had logged in his records.

Now what was it Sean had written, something to do with Wyman? No…It wasn't him, so who was it?

Although she racked her brains she could not remember. There was one thing for sure she knew, she wanted to help Richard but to do so she needed someone else to help her. She also needed to check back through Sean's papers to find what she was looking for.

"Richard," Richard paused and looked up from his meal, "going back to what you said in the other room, I've been thinking and I will help…"

"Great, I felt sure you would." There was sheer relief in his voice. It was music to his ears and his eyes danced with delight at hearing Jean's offer of help. "We need to draw up a plan of campaign, how we go forward, who we need to speak to…"

"Not so fast Richard. I'll help but I can't do it on my own."

The idea of enlisting other people may not be such a great idea Jean!

"Great. Thanks Jean." He paused. "Only one question, who are you going to get to help?"

"I thought I would get Jimmy on board."

I'm not too sure about Jimmy. Jimmy, Wyman either of these two could be Thief! I don't like it.

"Hmm. I'm not sure…" The exuberance in Richard's voice slowly subsided as he realised what she had said

"Why aren't you sure?" she asked him.

"Well…just a feeling that's all."

Well Richard you need to forget your gut feeling, because Jimmy is the best around and I'm not sure I can do it without him.

"Oh come on Richard. You know Jimmy; he's the best and completely trustworthy. Trust me on this one I know he's right and I know I'm right." Richard wasn't convinced.

"What happens if you're wrong Jean?"

"Well if I'm wrong then we have a major problem, but I'm certain that I'm not wrong. Anyway let's change the subject. There was something Sean had said…"

"What Jean?" Richard asked eagerly.

"I'm not too sure. I know that at the time it didn't make much sense to me but he logged it down somewhere. If only I can find that reference then I think we may have something."

"What do you think it could be?" Richard asked. "Is it about a place or do you think it's about a person?"

"Oh Richard, I'm not sure. It could be anything. The only thing I'm sure about is that it is nothing to do with Jimmy; he is as sound as they come," she said with feeling. "Anyway I need to go through Sean's papers before I do anything." Richard thought carefully about what she said, weighing up the pros and cons, was Jimmy *Thief*? In the end he had to admit that there was no evidence to support his mistrust of Jimmy, after all it was Jimmy who had frequently helped him in the past. Also Jimmy had been his greatest help in finding Jean and sorting out the two toerags who crawled out of the woodwork and got caught snooping around the yard.

You're right Jean I have no reason to mistrust him.

"All right Jean, Jimmy it is."

His mind wandered back to his encounter with Seamus and how he had been bound and gagged by him. It still puzzled him as to why Seamus had done what he did, and another thing that nagged at the back of his mind was Fionnuala, what had happened to her?

Perhaps you might know what's happened to Fionnuala Jean?

"There's one other thing Jean…"Jean gave a half hearted smile.

Now what? I thought we'd done Jimmy to death!

"What is it?" she asked half expecting some further argument about using Jimmy, but was completely taken aback by Richard's next question.

"Well, actually it is two questions…first of all did you know or do you know a contact in the 'circus' called Seamus O'Hare?" Jean thought about it for a while then shook her head.

"I can't say I do," she lied, "but there again I may know him by a codename. What does he look like?"

"Seamus O'Hare was a codename. I think he was originally based in Antrim and was moved near to the Tara. He used to be slim about average height, but like us all he has put a little weight on, but nothing to speak of. Age, about early forties, the first time I met him he was mid to late thirties; yes definitely early forties I'd say. Curly fair hair but thinning at the front. Sharp featured individual and gives the impression of being rather meek and mild. Sometimes he wears spectacles to add to this image, but there's nothing wrong with his twenty-twenty vision, the specs are plain glass and for effect only."

Jean thought about the man's description. Her brow furrowed as she appeared to mentally tick off various individuals in the 'circus'.

Of course I know Seamus. It's Kenny, he was living in Antrim? He had fair curly hair. Wasn't very tall either. A friend of Sean's until he was moved. Now who was his control?

"From your description it sounds like a guy who Sean once knew, he was living in Antrim, but not from there. He was there for a while then out of the blue he suddenly disappeared. He upped sticks and left. Rumour had it that he moved back to England, but then that was only a rumour. Sean said he'd heard that he was operating in County Louth somewhere."

"Where did Sean hear that?"

I wonder if Seamus is Kenny then.

"I'm not too sure but I think it was something Eamonn had said."

"Do you know who handled him?"

"Eamonn do you mean?"

"No Seamus, Kenny or whatever his name was or is?"

"No sorry Richard, may be Eamonn could help you on that one."

May be Jean, may be.

Silence ensued only to be broken by the faint noise from the central heating boiler as it kicked into life. Jean was the first to speak.

"You said that you had two questions, what was the other one?"

"Actually you've indirectly answered it. I was going to ask if it was you who had cut me free, but it couldn't have been because if you had you would definitely have known where Seamus or Kenny lived. You have already intimated that Sean lost touch with him once he moved. In fact it was only a rumour, so you said, and that he had moved to County Louth. Well Jean if this Kenny is Seamus, and I've no reason to doubt it is, I can confirm that he is very much alive and kicking and is indeed living in the Louth area."

Having partly satisfied his curiosity about who had rescued him Richard decided to let the matter drop and the discussion turned to the reason for Richard's visit and how Jean and Jimmy could help. They talked deep into the night, plotting and planning their way forward until eventually they had a skeleton of a plan. It was decided that Richard would return to Kent and wait for Jean to make contact. In the meantime Jean would check out her late husband's records and logs to see what, if anything, would throw light on the present situation. She felt that there was definitely something he had recorded somewhere that was a key to this whole situation. In addition to this it was agreed that she would contact Jimmy and talk to him and hopefully get him on board.

"How soon will you get back to me?" Richard asked.

"It will take me as long as it takes. I need to check through Sean's papers and find some documents. I then need to meet with Jimmy after I've done everything else. You're just going to have to trust me on this one."

"So how will I know whether or not Jimmy is on board?"

"Oh you'll know all right." Jean grinned, "I'll send you a post card."

"You are joking of course?"

"Of course I am Richard, of course I am."

I bet you are, because it's just the sort of thing you would do Mrs O'Donald!

"Don't worry Richard you'll know soon enough." With that she got up and glanced up at the clock, "Good God, it's nearly three o'clock. I don't know about you Richard James but I'm going to bed." Eventually completely exhausted, drained and brain dead they dragged their weary bodies up the stairs to bed.

Chapter 8

Although Richard had promised Jean that he would go back home to Kent, he had other ideas. An overnight stay at the Tara may help to answer a few questions, such as what had happened to Fionnuala and where had she gone? His thoughts turned back the years to when he first visited the area.

Ah yes Fionnuala – my beautiful Fionnuala what a time we had together – where are you now my lovely one?

For a moment or two he dwelled on the images of her smiling face. He imagined her here with him now, her laughter, her lilting Irish accent, her smiling blue eyes and her long flowing hair. These and many other pictures flashed through his mind's eye.

Are you married or still free and single?

The question remained unanswered. Then the thought occurred to him that may be Fionnuala's brother Danny had told her something that may well have a bearing on what had happened and this, he felt, was justification enough for staying at the Tara rather than keeping his promise to Jean.

Having already telephoned ahead Richard was secure in the knowledge that there was a room for him at the Tara and at four o'clock in the afternoon he checked in.

"Will you be dining with us tonight Mr James?"

"Yes thank you."

"At what time would you like a table?"

"May I let you know?"

"Of course you can Mr James. Is there anything else I can do for you?" she asked in an amiable way. *I wonder if Noel still works here,* Richard thought to himself.

"Yes, there is one thing," he asked. "Does Noel still work here?"

"Do you mean the night porter?" Richard nodded. "Yes he does sir. He comes on duty at seven-thirty." She smiled and went back to busying herself with sorting out paperwork.

"Excuse me," Richard once again attracted the young lady's attention. She looked up from what she was doing and smiled.

"Yes sir."

"There is one more thing." She looked at him with interest. "Do you or did you know a young lady called Fionnuala who used to work here?" The young lady thought for a moment or two.

"I think I do, a pretty girl…" Richard cut her short.

"Yes that's right, with long hair."

"Well if it is who I think it is, she was here when I first started, but she left some time ago."

"Oh," he said with feigned surprise, "I am surprised. When did she actually leave?"

"Ooh let me think," she paused to think back then shook her head, "I'm not certain, but it must be over a year. It may even be two years time flies so."

"Oh dear and a mutual friend gave me a package to deliver to her." He tried to sound genuinely disappointed at the news. "I don't suppose you have an address for her do you?" Richard asked tentatively hoping the young receptionist would fall for his ploy as he flashed a disarming smile.

"I'm sorry sir I haven't," she said returning the smile. Richard turned to go then as if it was an after thought he added, "I wonder, does the hotel have an address or telephone number for her, it's really important that I get this package to her," he lied. The receptionist smiled sweetly but shook her head. *Right, how about if I told you the area?* Richard thought to himself. "I know that her family used to live in Corke Abbey, may be that would help?"

"I'm sorry sir it doesn't help, and even if it did it would be more than my job's worth to give it to you."

Damn.

He stood there for a moment or two longer hoping that she might change her mind.

"Is there anything else sir?" she asked politely.

"No thank you and thanks anyway, it was worth a try." With that he picked up his overnight bag, smiled and made his way to the stairs. *Never mind,* he thought to himself, *hopefully Noel will turn something up.*

After a quick shower to freshen up from his drive, Richard decided to take a walk up the lane towards Breandán O'Shea's farm. As he turned out of the Hotel's driveway and into the tree lined lane his thoughts drifted back to a warm summer's day in the 1970s.

The birds were in full voice and dragonflies flitted to and fro in the hedgerow. The fields and orchards were lush and green and the sun was warm on his face. Ahh yes it was a lovely day. She was pretty. What was her name? I don't know Richard, you made love and never did know her name.

He smiled to himself as he thought about that particular afternoon. It was certainly different, the weather was warm and balmy not like today, cool and autumnal with the evenings drawing in and the leaves on the trees turning colour. Ahh yes it was different. He started to whistle. The tune that sprang to mind was *'Gentle on my mind'.*

'Hello there, it's a grand day for a walk isn't it?' She smiled at me and I replied, 'Yes it's beautiful.' She invited me in for coffee and I accepted. We listened to records, and I put on 'Gentle on my mind'...

He suddenly realised the tune he was whistling and stopped.

We made wild passionate love on her floor. Hmm that was a very special afternoon, I wonder what happened to her?'

He started to hum. The humming turned into a song and suddenly he found himself singing 'Come on, come on. Come on, come on come on. Do ya wanna be in my gang my gang my gang? Do you wanna be in my gang? Oh yeah…' He found himself singing the Gary Glitter song as he had done on that fateful day.

Ahh that was certainly a day to remember. Then she turned out to be IRA! Still you can't win them all.

Gradually he found himself repeating all the old songs he had sung; the Beatles medley was the next on the list. It may well have been coincidence but as he reached the bend in the lane he was on the chorus line and singing with gusto, *'I wanna hold your hand,'* when something very strange happened, a woman's voice joined in with the next line. He immediately stopped dead in his tracks, stopped singing and listened.

Can it be?

Yes there it was again. It was definitely someone singing the song 'I wanna hold your hand' and more to the point it was a voice that he recognised. He moved over to the low hedge and looked over. There she was that very same nurse, from back in the '70s, in the garden doing some tidying up.

"It is you!" he said incredulously. She looked over to the hedge and smiled.

"Yes, it is me. Hello Richard, it's been a long time hasn't it?" Her eyes twinkled mischievously as she asked, "would you like some coffee?" Talk about déjà vu this had to be more than a coincidence!

"Thank you I would love a coffee," he answered, then unable to contain himself any longer he immediately burst out laughing.

"What's the joke?" she asked a little tetchily unaware of what he had just been thinking.

"Nothing…" he spluttered trying hard to control his mirth, "nothing honestly. It's just me," he said as he momentarily gained his composure and stood there with a silly grin of disbelief on his face.

"I...I ..." he stuttered and stammered, and once again started to laugh.

"I what? Come on Richard tell me, you're not being fair what is the joke?" she asked again sounding even tetchier than the last time.

"Nothing honestly, it's just that...well, it's just that I can't believe it. There I was thinking to myself that the last time I came along here...well you know what I'm going to say anyway. And yes I would like some coffee." He grinned mischievously, "incidentally have you still got the album *'Gentle on my mind'*?" he asked. She now understood the reason for his merriment and felt her cheeks colour up as she realised the implication of his question.

"Maybe..." she answered somewhat coyly.

"Then coffee it shall be..."

The flames of the fire flickered gently casting long shadows on the walls of the cottage. She got up and pulled the curtains partially closed, switched on the two small table lamps that were situated on the window sills and the room was bathed in a gentle glow of yellow light.

"By the way how do you know my name?" Richard asked.

"Ah, I've known your name for a long time," she said without answering the question.

"What's your name, I never did know?"

"My name's Eleanor and yes I am still a nurse, well that's my cover anyway."

"How do you mean cover?"

"Surely you have realised it by now, I work for Sir James the same as you Richard." A frown furrowed Richard's brow, this contradicted everything he had thought all this time.

So why were you present at Breandán O'Shea's house talking with the O'Shea brothers when they were discussing keeping Thomas Niedermayer sedated at the clinic in Belfast and what have you got to do with their set-up?

"So how long have you worked for Sir James?"

"A long time, from about 1970 or thereabouts. Believe it or not I am a fully trained nurse. So it seemed logical that if I was to be used to obtain information on the IRA then what better way was there than to work as a nurse in a Belfast clinic owned then and still owned today by the O'Shea family, especially when Breandán O'Shea and his brother James are both known to be leading members of the Official IRA."

"So if you were working for Sir James then why wasn't anything done about Mr Niedermayer?"

"Ah, now that's a tricky one." She paused for a moment, "unfortunately I could not say anything about him because they, the O'Shea brothers and the IRA, would have known who had given them away and my cover would have been blown and that, dear Richard, would have been that. So you see I just had to keep quiet and the rest, as we say, is history." As she leant across him to pick up his dirty coffee cup her hair gently brushed against the side of his face. There it was again, that faint smell of perfume, a smell that Richard recognised from somewhere else. Then realisation dawned.

It was her. She was the one who had come to his rescue over at Seamus O'Hare's farm, or was his name Kenny. What did it matter Seamus, Kenny or it could be Jack the Ladd for all he cared. So she was his saviour. Then how did she know he was at the farm?

"More coffee Richard?"

"Yes please…You're the one!"

"I'm the one what?"

"You're the one who set me free over at the farm aren't you?" She didn't have to say anything; she just gave a knowing smile. "How did you know I was there?" he asked.

"Because..." she started to say then changed her mind, "let's just say I had heard."

"Not good enough." Richard's eyes narrowed as he waited for her explanation. "I need to know how you knew I was there," he insisted, but she still remained steadfastly silent. "Was I set-up by Sir James?" he suddenly asked.

"Of course not..." she said with indignation.

"Well how come I was sandbagged by Seamus?"

"Well," she paused and thought carefully about her answer. "Seamus is a good operator, but like a lot of people in the 'circus' he was misinformed. He was told that you were unreliable, that you had had a breakdown and that you were a security risk." She watched Richard's face closely but he was impassive. "As you know in this game, bad news always travels fast. So, when he heard about Rosie and that you had been to visit her he assumed that you had something to do with her demise. Then of course he found you at the farm which left him with no alternative but to immobilise you and report back." Richard was puzzled by Eleanor's last remark about Rosie.

So where does Rosie fit in with all this and how does her elimination tie in with Seamus?

"But what has Rosie's death to do with Seamus?" he asked.

"Ah Richard, my dear Richard, surely you knew about Rosie and Seamus?" There was a look of puzzlement in Richard's eyes that said it all.

"No not at all, what about Seamus and Rosie?" His question confirmed what she had suspected, that Richard was totally unaware that Rosie was his handler and rumour was at one time she had been more than just his handler.

"So you never knew Rosie was his handler then?"

"I'm damned if I did! Well I suppose that explains why he reacted like he did, but you said he had to report back...with Rosie dead who was her back-up?"

"Fortunately it's Eamonn…"

"Why fortunately?"

"Because Eamonn works very closely with Jimmy."

That's no recommendation. Hmm I don't totally trust Jimmy. I wonder who he is working for; perhaps you know something I don't?

"Jimmy you say." Eleanor nodded. "So what do you know about Jimmy?" Richard sat back in his chair, his head back with eyes half closed and listened patiently to Eleanor as she explained the background to the current set-up in the 'circus'. Seamus had been out of the farm for some months, away on another project, but had recently rejoined the Irish sector. Rosie and Seamus had been very close friends for many years, but eventually other projects came along and they lost touch with each other until the late 1970s when once again they worked together. Rosie had been the contact for Seamus when the Dublin project was being put together and became his handler at the time of the bombing in Dublin. Some time after the Dublin bombing he was moved to another project so the farm was vacated for a time. Eventually he returned to operations in Ireland and after a short period of familiarisation up in Lisburn he returned to sector. During his time in Lisburn he had heard whispers about Richard, about his arrest back in the UK.

Very soon the rumours were that the operator known as Ferryman had had a breakdown and had been admitted to a psychiatric unit. It became common knowledge that Ferryman, one of the top operators, had become a major security risk and should be avoided at all cost. This was the party line put out by the department and very soon Richard's name became synonymous with 'security risk' and 'breakdown'. He was not to be trusted and as if to reinforce the party line the news of an operator's death in the twenty-six counties was quickly linked to Richard. When Seamus found Richard asleep at the boarded-up farm some forty-eight hours later he was placed on the horns of a dilemma. Although he had heard the various stories put out by the department about Ferryman, the arrest and the breakdown, he had also heard other whispers which had seemed to have gained momentum. There was talk of a 'scapegoat', a 'mole' at high level and a 'set-up', nothing really concrete, but nevertheless there is no smoke without fire. Fortunately the rumours about Richard had instilled sufficient doubt in the mind of Seamus to warrant him putting a question mark against the official party line. It was for this very reason that although Seamus had followed the party line he didn't believe that there was any connection between Richard's visit and Rosie's death, and in her absence Seamus contacted Eamonn his back-up contact and handler.

Upon receipt of a coded red message Eamonn arranged to meet with Seamus at the Border Inn, set deep in the woods off the road known as the 'butter run', a road that had been used for many years by the Official IRA. Because Seamus had misgivings about Richard's guilt, he made a slight detour en route to meet Eamonn and called in to see Eleanor. On the pretence that he had some urgent business to attend to 'up country' he asked her to collect a package he had left over on the boarded up farm.

"I presume that I was the package," Richard said looking straight at Eleanor.

"Yes that's right. Fortunately I took the hint and went over to the farm to investigate and I found you."

"But where does Jimmy fit into all of this?"

"Well it was Jimmy who recommended you to Sir James. You see Jimmy now works over in the Irish Sector in London, but unknown to them he is also with us working directly for Sir James. So you can rest assured that Jimmy is an ally should you ever need one."

Well, I'll be damned, he thought to himself, *so Jimmy is working for Sir James, which means that he is definitely not Thief. Now that certainly <u>does</u> make a difference.*

Richard drummed with his fingers on the arm of the chair as he tried to make sense of it all. *Things are never straightforward.*

"So let me get this straight. One, you work for Sir James..." he glanced at Eleanor. She nodded. "Two, Jimmy works for Sir James but is also in the Irish Sector London..." he paused. "So where does Seamus fit in?"

"Seamus works for Intelligence, through Eamonn now..."

"So who does Eamonn work for?"

"Military Intelligence."

"But doesn't Jimmy?" Richard asked.

"Yes and no. He was always MI6, but he has been in the armed forces and actively involved with military intelligence. He is now part of our team and works directly for Sir James."

"So how many are there?"

"Not many, but I'm not too sure, there is one more piece of information you may like to know."

"What's that?"

Eleanor put a finger to her lips indicating for him to be quiet then taking hold of his hand she gently pulled him from his chair.

"Come... follow me."

Holding his hand tightly she lead him up the stairs and into the bedroom. As they entered the room Richard gave a sharp intake of breath for there, staring back at him, was a neatly framed picture of himself standing on a yacht. Although the picture had been taken quite some time ago, he remembered it well.

The sea looked cool and inviting as it slipped beneath the bow of the yacht. The only sound, apart from a lone seagull's cry, was the gentle 'swish' made by the yacht as it sliced through the calmness of the sea. Fionnuala, her body golden brown from the sun, looked beautiful as she lay there sunbathing.

"What the…"

But before he could say anything further Eleanor thrust something into his hand. It was a photograph album. In a slight daze, he opened the album. The first page was of him in the grounds of the hotel where he had stayed the night with Fionnuala. He flicked over to the next page, another photograph, and the next page the same. He started to turn over the pages more and more quickly. Each time it showed different photographs of him.

How has she got these and why?

He glanced quickly at Eleanor then back at the album in his hand.

"What the hell are you doing with my photographs in your bedroom?" he asked her angrily. She didn't reply, instead she grabbed hold of his hand and half dragged and half manoeuvred him to the chest of drawers where a large picture of Danny, Fionnuala's brother stared back at him.

"Don't you see Richard…?"

"See what? All I see is that you have…or should I say Sir, bloody James has obtained photographs of me…or someone has and given them to you. Why?"

"You just don't get it do you?" Eleanor retaliated angrily. She was annoyed with his childish outburst.

"Get what?" he asked a look of puzzlement on his face. His sudden outburst of anger gradually subsided and once more he appeared to be the reasonably calm Richard James she knew. "Get what?" he asked again in a quieter voice.

"The photographs. Look again and ask yourself why or who would have these in their bedroom. It certainly isn't me."

"I...I thought this was your bedroom." Slowly realization dawned.

Oh shit. What a fool I've been...yes now I see it.

"Are you saying Fionnuala is here, right here living with you?" Richard asked trying hard to stay calm in light of his recent findings. Eleanor nodded and smiled. Richard suddenly felt all the old feelings stirring deep inside as he remembered the nights they had together.

Is that her perfume I can smell? Oh Fionnuala I can just picture you now, your long hair falling about your shoulders – how you gave a little toss of your head and laughed. How your eyes twinkled mischievously. Yes I can imagine you here with me now.

He looked around the bedroom taking in every last detail.

"So where is she?"

"She had to go back home to Corke Abbey because her mother hasn't been very well, but she's better now and she should be back late tonight."

In that case perhaps I'll stay for a few more days before going home.

"I presume she isn't or should I say didn't get married then."

"No she is still single. I think you were her true love really."
A puzzled look crossed Richard's face. There was one thing bothering him. If she was living here and not working at the Tara, then where did she get her income? Did this mean she was also part of the 'circus'?

There was a spring in his step as Richard walked the short distance from the gate to the front door of the cottage. He reached up to the heavy wrought iron knocker and gave three sharp knocks and waited. He waited and listened for the slightest sound of movement from inside the cottage but heard nothing. Everywhere was still, nothing stirred. Even the slight breeze had dropped. There was silence save for the singing of a single bird. A puzzled look crossed his face.

Strange, Eleanor told me Fionnuala was returning last night.

He gave three more sharp knocks and waited. Still silence. Even the sole bird had stopped singing. He was beginning to worry.

Have I been stupid all along? Has the lovely Eleanor set me up?

He casually glanced around the front of the cottage. All the windows were closed tight and there was no apparent sign of life. His mind made up he moved off in the direction of the back of the cottage.

The path from the back door led to a small gate that opened out straight into the woods to the rear. These were the very same woods that were alarmed and ran from the Tara Hotel through to O'Shea's place. They were the very same alarmed woods that he, Richard James, had negotiated in the middle of the night to spy on Breandán O'Shea. They were the same alarmed woods that he had taken Kenneth Austen through when he delivered him to the safe house north of the border. So nobody knew these woods better than Richard James. The back of the cottage was, like the front, closed up completely. He tentatively tried the door, but it was locked. He knocked at the back door but held out little hope of getting a reply – he was right. His buoyant mood slowly evaporated as he came to the conclusion that he was on a wild goose chase and with a shrug of his shoulders he decided to call it a day and set off to walk back through the woods that he knew so well.

He had only been walking for a matter of minutes when he caught a glimpse of someone through the trees. His immediate action was to stop and conceal himself. Old habits die hard. He pressed his body back into the rhododendron bushes where he was adequately concealed and stood there stock still as he watched the area up ahead, listening intently for the slightest noise, or hoping to catch a glimpse of the slightest movement. He waited concealed in the bushes for what seemed like an indeterminable length of time, but it paid off. Over to his left there was the snap of a twig, not far away from his hiding place. He could now hear their breathing. Whoever it was, was heading his way. He now judged them to be very close to his position, but because they were the other side of the clump of rhododendrons he couldn't get a view of them. He waited, and waited. He could now hear their breathing. He held his breath and pressed further back into the bush. Another snap of a branch or twig announced that they were now directly opposite him on the other side of the bush and heading towards the cottage. Again the thought that he may have been setup by Eleanor entered his head.

Shall I jump them, or just wait and follow?

Whoever it was had now passed and the sound of their breathing was growing fainter.

I'm sure they are heading for the cottage. Another few minutes then my friend I'll surprise you.

He counted up to sixty, and then quickly and stealthily he moved off to follow his quarry. In a matter of minutes he had covered the distance back to the gate of the cottage.

If I've judged this right I should be able to be inside the gate and conceal myself sufficiently enough to grab them as they enter.

Even though his earlier cursory look around the back of the cottage had only taken a moment or two, with Richard's background it had proved long enough for him to ascertain the house was deserted and that there was sufficient cover to the right of the open gate for him to secrete himself away from prying eyes. Also the cover afforded was close enough for him to have the element of surprise necessary in order for him to apprehend his victim.

Having managed to secrete himself away, it still left him with one problem, and that was he hadn't got a good line of sight so the face of whoever it was would be obscured from his view. As he waited in his hideaway he could hear the sound of approaching footsteps. He craned his neck to try and get a better line of sight but to no avail. He held his breath as the footsteps came closer. A dark shadow fell across his hideaway as whoever it was drew level then they passed and the footsteps started to recede. Stealthily Richard moved from his hiding place and with the speed and agility of a cat he sprung through the air towards his target, hitting the back of the male intruder fair and square. The force of the impact knocked the would-be intruder off his feet completely, the very breath forced from his body as he landed with a thud face down on the path.

Right my old son, now let's get a look at your face.
The stranger groaned as Richard roughly manhandled him onto his back.

"It's you!" Richard couldn't believe it. "What the hell…" The victim, with the stuffing knocked out of him, stared up at Richard. Then as he slowly recovered his breath recognition dawned.

"Jesus Mr James…I mean Richard, what t'fuck did yer do that for?" Richard stared back at the man's body beneath him realising his mistake.

"I'm sorry Noel, a slight case of mistaken identity. Here let me give you a hand up." With an outstretched hand he helped Noel get back on his feet.

"B'jesus Richard yer fairly frightened me that's fer sure," Noel said as he brushed the dirt from his clothes, "and what d'yer mean by a 'case of mistaken identity' and all that?"

"It's a long story Noel and not for repeating now… so how are you keeping?"

"Oh I'm keeping fine."

"You're still working at the Tara then."

"To be sure I am. I still need to earn a crust."

I bet you are and I bet you are still making a few bob on your evening drinks tabs!

Their conversation was interrupted by a woman's voice.

"Noel, is that you?" Richard immediately recognised Fionnuala's voice.

"To be sure it's me, who else would it be?" Noel called back.

"I just wondered…" Fionnuala appeared from around the side of the cottage…"Who are you talking to…?" She saw Richard and stopped dead in her tracks, her mouth worked but nothing came out. 'Who…what…Richard it is you.' All thoughts of Noel vanished as she ran to Richard. "Richard James, I thought I would never see you again." She threw her arms round him and kissed him passionately. Embarrassed by her own actions she quickly broke away and looked sheepishly at the ground. She could feel herself colouring up as she said, "I'm sorry, I don't know what came over me."

To be sure you didn't know what came over you; if you think I believe that then you must have kissed the blarney stone. Go tell that to the little people.

Noel stole a quick look at Richard and thought; *even you look a shade embarrassed by that little display.* He cleared his throat. "Well Fionnuala aren't you going to invite us in for a cup of tea or something?" He winked at Richard.

"Yes…yes of course." She said, desperately trying to overcome her embarrassment caused through her impetuous action. "How rude of me, yes please do come in and Richard you can tell me what's been happening since I last saw you."

Having now regained her composure Fionnuala led the way back around to the front of the cottage.

"Oh, is that the time?" Noel said as he looked at his watch, "I must go. Sorry Fionnuala I'll have to leave the tea," he said using his discretion, "I only popped up to say that Danny has been trying to get hold of you and asked me, to ask you, to phone him later today if you would."

Now why would Danny phone Noel at the Tara when there is a perfectly good phone here at the cottage?
Richard shot Noel a sideways glance.

"Is that why you were here then Noel?"

"Yes…"

"My phone's out of order." Fionnuala quickly interjected, "or should I say Eleanor's phone's out of order and we are waiting for it to be repaired so Noel acts as my messenger boy, don't you Noel?"

Sounds plausible.

"Yes of course." There was an uncomfortable pause. Noel gave a slight nervous cough, "well, I must go now or I'll never get things done. I'll see you later Fionnuala." He turned to Richard, "and what about you my friend, am I likely to see you?"

"I expect so Noel."

Richard took another sip of his tea and looked fondly at the beautiful Fionnuala his mind running riot.

You haven't changed a bit, still the same Fionnuala. Oh how I've missed you. You look just as good as you always did. You may be older but the years have been kind to you.

"I heard that you've had a hard time of things back in England, do you want to tell me about it?" she asked in a soft voice.

Richard, knowing that Fionnuala was the one person he could trust unreservedly, told her everything, well nearly everything. He just failed to tell her the main reason for his visit this time. In fact the way he put it was that he was on a flying visit, he was just passing through, on his way to price up some contract work further north. Gradually he turned the conversation round to Danny.

"Does Danny still work for C3 and the British Government?"

"Yes for the present, why?"

"Can you set up a meeting with Danny for me?"

"Hmm may be. Why?"

"I'm sorry I can't tell you now, but trust me, it's very important. Incidentally where were you this morning?"

"Don't change the subject, why do you want the meeting?"

"Sorry I can't say at the moment." He turned the question back to her. "So where were you this morning?"

"Why?"

"It's just that Eleanor said you were coming back late last night so I came up here earlier, but when I knocked at the door the place was deserted and yet you seemed to have been expecting Noel. What's going on Fionnuala, are you working with Eleanor and Danny?"

"How long have you known about Eleanor?" she asked.

"Oh a while." Richard lied. "So tell me are you working with Eleanor?" Just for a fleeting moment Fionnuala looked serious then the old Fionnuala returned. She made up her mind and nodded.

"Yes and no"

"Which is it Fionnuala, yes or no?" She sighed.

"All right." She sounded cross, "so I have been helping them out from time to time."

"So were you working for them when I was over here last time?" There was silence. Richard waited patiently but Fionnuala sat quietly examining her finger nails refusing to look up at him and refusing to say a word. In the end it was Richard who spoke first.

"Were you working for Eleanor and Danny when I was over here last time?" Richard repeated his question. Again silence. Again Richard repeated the question.

"Fionnuala I am asking you, were you working for Eleanor and Danny the last time I was here, if you don't answer me then I must assume you were?" Fionnuala lifted her gaze and looked Richard straight in the eyes. There was no mistaking her anger at being challenged by him and her eyes flashed with annoyance.

How dare you Richard James? Who are you to challenge me in this way?

"I don't work for them," she said her voice raised in anger. "I've never worked for them. I work for your people; I work with Danny and Eleanor not for them," she answered petulantly. "There I've told you." Once again she glowered at Richard then felt the tears start to well up in her eyes. She immediately looked away in order to conceal her feelings and the strain she had been under. The frustration of not being able to tell him before about her involvement, especially as she was aware of what he had gone through, was now beginning to tell. Richard, like Fionnuala, sat in silence wrapped up in his own thoughts.

If she is working with Danny and Eleanor then there is no reason why I shouldn't tell her what I'm up to over here. Besides at present she is the only one I can really trust.

"OK I'll come clean with you. As you know I think I was setup by the department, or somebody high up in the department and I am now trying to find out who it was. Will you help me?" Richard had decided to make it look personal so playing on her emotions. He needed her to help him find this mole. The only potential problem was Danny. If he was still passing info back to the UK then regardless of his viewpoints he could inadvertently be dangerous.

I need to get Danny on my side.

"Of course I will help you, but how?"

Richard explained how he felt that Danny could, without realising it, be putting him at risk and possibly putting his own life in jeopardy, and for that reason he needed her to set up a meeting between him and Danny. "It's imperative that you impress upon Danny that he doesn't tell anyone about this meeting – especially his handler. Make sure he knows that."

"OK, so where will you meet?"

"How about here?" Fionnuala thought about this for a moment or two before answering.

"Don't you think here's a bit... well close to...things?"

"What do you mean by things?"

"Well I was thinking about Seamus, the Tara and O'Shea."

Richard considered this for a few moments but decided that the risk was minimal to both himself and Danny.

"The chance of Seamus, O'Shea or anyone else finding out is really remote, but just as a precaution perhaps you and Eleanor should be here." Fionnuala pulled a face.

"That's not possible. Eleanor is at the clinic for the next two weeks."

"In which case just you."

"So what if anybody turns up?"

"Well if Danny and I meet in your bedroom, you can always stall whoever it is at the door."

"How do you propose I do that Mr James?" she asked with a mischievous glint in her eyes as she moved closer. The strain of the last few minutes had passed and she now felt like her old self once again and it showed. "Well..." she was now really close to him and before he could protest she threw her arms about his neck and cut him off mid sentence with a lingering kiss. It had been a long time since Richard had felt Fionnuala in such close proximity and it didn't take her long to rekindle that old feeling. She could feel his passion rising as she caressed his neck. She broke away from him and smiled mischievously and said, "did you mean like that Mr James?"

"Hmm…not what I quite had in mind." *God Fionnuala how I want you.* Richard slowly pulled her to him and resumed their passionate embrace. With one free hand he skilfully undid the buttons to her blouse and pushed it off first one shoulder, and then the other, and with a little help from Fionnuala the blouse dropped to the floor. In a trice he had undone the zip of her skirt and removed the last vestige of clothing. Her hands eagerly wrestled with his clothing, pulling and tugging in earnest as she removed his shirt and trousers. With inflamed passion they sank to the floor, his hands moving skilfully over her breasts and the contours of her body, touching her, caressing her very soul.

Hmm that feels good Richard James. It's been so long – too long. Please don't stop.

The phone just kept ringing and ringing.

Danny where are you? Just pick up the phone.

At last the ringing stopped and a male voice answered.

"Hello."

"Danny, at last where've you been…?"

"Who is that…?"

"B'jesus Danny don't you even recognise your own sister now?"

"Fionnuala what y…"

"Shh, listen Danny this is urgent." Danny detected the seriousness in her tone and immediately tensed up.

"What's wrong Fi…?" She cut him off in mid sentence.

"Just…just come over to my place tonight…"

"What's the problem?" he asked as he sensed something was wrong. His mind went into a whirl.

Have you been found out? Jesus I hope not – O'Shea can be a nasty bastard.

"No real problem...well...that is not yet anyway." She heard a sharp intake of breath and knew she must have sounded convincing. "Look Danny, you must come over..."

"What's wrong?" His voice had an edge to it.

If there's no problem then why are you so tense?

"I'll tell you later. Can't talk now...just need you here that's all. Promise me you'll come."

"Of course I will. In fact I'll leave straightaway...."

"Thanks Danny and Danny..."

"What?"

"Don't say a word about this to anyone..." A frown crept across his forehead. This was so unlike his sister he was now concerned.

"Did you hear me Danny?"

Now why doesn't she want me to say anything?

"Danny are you there?"

"Yeah, yes I'm still here. So why don't you want me to say anything to the others?"

"Can't say now but it will all fall into place when you get here. Just promise me you'll keep quiet on this one."

"OK...' he paused, 'but..."

"No 'buts' Danny. Just keep quiet or your life could be in jeopardy. Remember not a word, not even to control. I'll see you soon." There was a click and the line went dead. Danny stared at the handset in his hand, still not sure that he was doing the right thing by not informing control.

Fionnuala replaced the handset and turned to Richard somewhat concerned.

"Do you think I sounded convincing enough?"

"I think you sounded great. If I had been Danny I would have been convinced. I told you last night it would work. Well done. All we need to do now is to sit and wait for him to arrive. Don't forget, if anyone turns up after he's got here you come down and get rid of them. Perhaps you ought to get ready..."

"For bed...?" She raised an eyebrow in her quizzical way and laughed.

"You know what I mean. Just get into your night clothes and we'll wait for Danny." He gave her a playful smack as she passed by his chair and headed off upstairs.

Chapter 9

Paul glanced up at the clock. It was a little after nine and there was still no news from Richard. Nothing seemed to be happening. He wondered if Richard had made any progress over in Ireland.

Perhaps he ought to phone the Tara and see if he was there. Hmm, then what? Perhaps not such a good idea after all, you'll just have to be patient.

Suddenly the chimes of the front doorbell brought him back to the present with a jolt.

Now I wonder who that can be.

His mind went back to that fateful night in the workshop when he had a visit from his three erstwhile attackers, and not taking any chances – if nothing else it had taught him to be somewhat more cautious than before – he carefully pulled aside one of his sitting room curtains in order to get a clear view of his front door. At the same time he was careful to remain back from the window. After all he did not wish to experience a similar attack to that of Richard's when he got shot at in the psychiatric unit. He could just about see the front door from where he stood and was surprised to see Johnny Rains on the doorstep.

What on earth could you want Johnny?

Paul carefully scrutinised Johnny Rains for a moment or two longer. He was still unsure of the man; especially as it transpired that it was through him going to the Police that fateful night that he and Richard had been arrested. No he wasn't sure of him at all. Paul screwed up his eyes and peered as far as he could see looking for the slightest tell-tale movement. He wanted to make sure that Mr Rains was all alone before he opened the front door. No last minute rushes for him from concealed bodies. No sir, he had been down that road before. The chimes of the front door rang again.

All right, all right I'm coming.

Paul undid the front door.

"Johnny," he said with mock surprise. "What a surprise, what brings you here?"

Yeah I wonder what or should I say who brings you here?

"Come in." He held the door open for Johnny Rains. Johnny glanced nervously about him before entering Paul's house.

My you seem nervous Johnny.

"To what do I owe this unexpected pleasure?" Paul enquired as he led him through into his sitting room. "Please sit down." He indicated the nearby easy chair in front of the window. "Would you like a cup of tea Johnny, or a beer?"

"I'm driving so a cup of tea will be fine thank you Paul." Johnny Rains looked nervous and very much on edge as he sat in the chair. He certainly felt ill at ease, which was no wonder after his last experience when he met up with Paul. That night would remain vivid in his mind's eye for the rest of his days and the threats had up until now kept him very much in check. But tonight he had made a decision for whatever reason to tell Paul what had happened.

"Milk and sugar Johnny?" Paul called to him from the kitchen.

"Umm...no...no...no thanks, sorry... sugar, no sugar I mean," he answered nervously.

Come on John pull yourself together Paul's on your side. He's not the enemy.

"Here we are then." Paul placed two mugs of tea on the coffee table. "So what brings you here?" Johnny picked up the mug of freshly made tea and took a sip.

"I'm sorry Paul; if it's inconvenient I can leave it."

"No not at all."

Of course it's bloody inconvenient but more to the point why are you here?

"So what's the problem?" Johnny looked at Paul and nervously chewed at his thumbnail as he did. He then looked down at the floor unable to look straight at Paul and mumbled something about being kidnapped the night they had met at the pub.

"Did I hear you right Johnny, did you say someone grabbed you outside the Eight Bells the night you met up with me?" Johnny nodded his head. "What did they want Johnny?" he asked, but Johnny Rains just shrugged his shoulders and stared down at his feet. "Well man, tell me, what did they want?" Paul asked angrily.

"I... I'm not sure," Johnny stammered unconvincingly. "It...it all happened so quickly...they just grabbed me, tied me up, blindfolded me and bundled me into a car and...and..."

"And what?"

"And drove off..." he answered lamely and in a voice little more than a whisper.

Come on Paul it's no good bullying the man he looks shit scared. So what's he scared of? Good question, I wonder...

"How many of them did you say there were?" Paul asked softly.

"Three," Johnny answered. "Yes, there were three of them," he repeated somewhat more confidently.

Hmm, I wonder if the three visitors I had at the workshop and this episode are connected, I wouldn't mind betting that they are.

"So you had better start right at the beginning Johnny and tell me the full story," Paul said softly as he settled further back in his armchair and with eyes half closed he listened carefully to Johnny's story. Johnny went over the story of his kidnap in every last detail, only stopping occasionally to take a mouthful of tea, or to answer some question posed by Paul. Every now and then Paul would ask him to repeat something. Having now told Paul the full story Johnny looked a lot less nervous than he had upon arrival, but had he known the truth about Paul and Richard it may have changed the whole sequence of events.

The clock on the mantelpiece said nine o'clock when there was a gentle tap at the front door. Richard eased the curtain back just sufficiently to give him a clear view of the front door of the cottage. He heard Fionnuala's footsteps overhead as she went to her bedroom window to do the same thing. The trace of a slight smile briefly touched his lips as he envisaged his lovely Fionnuala dressed in her night clothes and ready to feign ill health should an unwelcome visitor come calling. He craned his neck to see who was there. It was Danny all right and he was alone. Richard moved to a position behind the door, knowing full well that Danny would let himself in if his knock went unanswered. Fionnuala was under strict instructions to remain out of sight and upstairs in her bedroom. Richard had impressed upon her that it was imperative that he should see Danny before they all met in her bedroom, convincing her that there were some things he needed to discuss with him first. He waited with bated breath but still Danny remained outside.

What's the problem Danny – come on come in, or do you know I'm here?

There was another tap at the door.

Perhaps he has seen Fionnuala at her window. Damn you Fionnuala get back from the window.

Time seemed to stand still as Richard waited for Danny to come in, then he saw the door handle move. Every sinew and every muscle in Richard's body tensed as he steeled himself for the inevitable opening of the door. The door slowly opened.

Come on Danny, just a little wider.

It was wider now and Danny cautiously stepped inside. Softly he called Fionnuala's name, but got no reply. The open door shielded Richard from view as Danny moved further into the room.

Just one more step and...

Suddenly the door slammed closed as Richard, catlike, sprang through the air grabbing Danny as he did so. Danny gave an involuntary gasp as he crashed to the floor where the last vestige of air was knocked from his body. The attack had completely taken Danny by surprise and Richard pressed home his advantage. He immediately put an arm lock on Danny and with a knee thrust between his shoulder blades he had very quickly and skilfully pinned him face down against the carpet, thus immobilising him completely. With his free hand Richard quickly and skilfully checked his victim's body for any sign of a weapon – he was unarmed.

"Right Danny boy lie still and listen to me." Richard whispered in his ear. "We need to talk about things. Things that concern both you and I. Things I need answers to and things that you need to know. Do I make myself clear?" Danny nodded. "Good. I'm going to let you go now and we are going to go upstairs to your sister's bedroom..."

"What have you done to her...?"

"Nothing. She's fine; she's upstairs waiting for us. Now just relax and answer my question, did you keep this meeting secret yes or no?"

"I did as I was asked, but if I'd have known you were here then..." He didn't finish the sentence before Richard let go of his arm and released him.

"OK Danny, come on I'll give you a hand to get up."

"Fuck off you bastard. I can get up myself. I know all about you, how you betrayed your colleagues when you were arrested, the lies and the desperate measures you took to cover your own arse..."

"Whoa Danny, not so fast...come on let's go upstairs and talk to your sister."

If only you knew the half of it Danny boy.

Danny pulled his arm away from Richard's helping hand and jumped to his feet. His annoyance clearly showed in the expression on his face. For a moment or two he stood glowering at Richard and for a fleeting second he even toyed with the idea of lashing out, but that soon passed. Angrily he spun round and stomped off up the stairs. Suddenly realisation dawned. Not only had he been jumped by Richard, but he had also been conned into this situation by his very own flesh and blood. There was no doubt in his mind that he had been well and truly duped by Fionnuala into meeting up with her and Richard.

What a fool I've been. Fancy letting my dear little sister con me into believing all that claptrap about my life being in jeopardy and all that.

"Danny, I'm pleased you c..."

"What are you doing in your night clothes?" he asked angrily.

Don't tell me, I can guess. You've been screwing this miserable piece of low life, this shit, this bastard.

"Just got up have you?" he asked sarcastically, "I hope I'm not interrupting anything?"

"Danny calm down and listen." Richard tried to reason with him but he was having none of it.

"B'jesus you English pig, why don't you just piss off?"

"But it's not what it seems. Just listen to yourself Danny, you're being totally unreasonable and childish. Richard works for Sir James..."

"Bollocks...I don't believe you."

"It's true Danny." Danny fell silent. He looked first at his sister then at Richard, then back at his sister.

"No...no...it's...that's crap...isn't it? Please tell me it is crap."

"Incredulous though it seems to you Danny, it's true. I do work for Sir James. Now please do as Fionnuala says. Please sit down and listen, and Danny, it was true what she said, your life could well be in danger." At last Danny calmed down and slowly and in incredulity he sank down on the bed. Richard motioned to Fionnuala to go and lock the front door just in case any uninvited guests turned up as he moved the stool from under the dressing table and sat down opposite Danny.

"The reason why your sister is in her night clothes is in case we get any unwanted visitors. The idea is that, should someone turn up at the front door then Fionnuala will make her excuses and say she is not very well and get them to call back another time, when she is better, and hopefully they will leave without question."

"So why up here in her bedroom?"

"Oh Danny, Danny use your head. We are up here in her bedroom for the very reason that I've just said, in case we get any unwanted visitors, and I need to get some answers for Sir James and pretty damn quick at that…"

"Why you?"

"It's a long story Danny and not for the telling right now."

"How do I know you are on the level, and what sort of things are you after?"

"I suppose you could always ask Sir James should you have a mind to."

"I'm sure I'm going to do that." Danny answered sarcastically.

"Well then you'll just have to trust me on that one Danny boy. Now think about it Danny, if I wasn't on your side I could have killed you the moment you walked in here."

"Hmm, I suppose so." Danny answered begrudgingly.

"Aw come on Danny. You know it's true and what's more I could have killed your sister." He could have bitten his tongue off for just at that precise moment Fionnuala returned from downstairs.

"Thank you very much Richard James and I love you too. I hope you didn't mean that?"

"Of course I didn't." He gave a little laugh. "Don't be silly I was only speaking figuratively. Now some of the things I need to know…for instance how well do you know Seamus Danny?"

"Reasonably, as well as anybody in this game I guess, why what about him?" Richard chose to ignore his question and pressed on with another question.

"Do you know his handler?"

"Why?" This time he decided to answer his question.

"Because I found out some information whilst I was snooping around the old farm. Incidentally how long has it been boarded up?"

"A long time, ever since you left the Tara isn't it Fionnuala?" Fionnuala nodded her head in agreement.

"That makes it about six months now. So what did you find over there?"

"Sorry Danny I can't tell you that. Tell me, do you know who his handler is?"

"Not really. It used to be someone in Lisburn; a woman I think. Rumour was that he got quite involved with her one way or another but that was a while back. I don't know whether he is still handled through Lisburn or whether it's someone else north of here."

"Who for example?"

"Perhaps Eamonn. I had heard rumours that he had handled someone in this neck of the woods." Richard sat and pondered on this last bit of information.

Do I need to visit Eamonn? Why or how is Eamonn involved… if Eamonn was something to do with Seamus that could explain…?

"So what's Seamus got to do with anything?" Danny's question brought Richard back to the present.

"I'm not too sure at the moment."

Do I tell Danny that I'd clocked him tailing me...perhaps not such a good idea...I'll let him think I hadn't seen him...Begs another question though do I mention Rosie and who is your handler Danny, is it still Mr Wyman?

"Tell me Danny, who handles you nowadays?"

"You know very well who I'm handled by – it's Wyman of course and you know it is."

"Sorry Danny of course, it must be old age, it err...just slipped my mind that's all."

So if Wyman handles you and was Austen's handler, then who handled Rosie? Was she handled through Ashford or through the Ambassador's Office here in Dublin?

"Who else does Wyman handle, any ideas?" Richard tried to make his question sound as casual as possible.

"I had heard on the grapevine that he had handled Eamonn at one time but I'm not sure."

So I was right! Wyman handles Austen, you Danny boy and Eamonn. Eamonn handles Seamus, or does he? If he does then is that the link...could that be why Seamus ...so who can be trusted?

The more Danny talked, the more Wyman seemed to crop up in the conversation and a picture started to emerge. Like a video, pictures were conjured up in Richard's brain, images dredged from the past flickered in his mind's eye.

Seamus, that skilled explosives expert, the man I trusted, could well be handled by Eamonn, who was in turn handled by Wyman at one time. Wyman handles Danny and he also handled Austen. Eamonn was my contact whilst I worked for O'Shea here in the South. It was Wyman who provided the intelligence with Danny on the abortive raid on Riley's farm so does that make Wyman 'Thief'. Hmm, I certainly need to get in touch with Sir James and quickly, but who can be trusted?

One by one Richard started to mentally tick off the people he felt he could trust and so far they were few and far between.

Rosie – she's dead! Jean she's in Lisburn. Possibly Eleanor, but she was somewhere in the North. The British Embassy in Dublin – but that's only useful to contact Sir James in an emergency - and then there is you, my lovely Fionnuala. The Ambassador's Office could be used if Sir James were to arrange it. May be Eamonn was worth a visit, perhaps he could be of help?

Silence descended on the small party congregated in the bedroom of the cottage.

In all of this Wyman was the common denominator.

'Jock screamed in pain as we manoeuvred him into a sitting position. Wyman crouched down at the other side, pulled Jock's arm over his shoulder, slipped his arm around Jock's waist, and I did likewise,' it was Wyman who had extricated both Richard and Jock from the abortive raid on 'slab' Riley's farm.

It was Wyman who had been with him in the safe house when it was attacked and they both had very nearly been killed.

The front door burst open and there was running along the passage. Both Wyman and I grabbed our weapons and before the door opened we opened fire.

That day the safe house was attacked, and like the rescue from Riley's farm it was indelibly printed on Richard's memory, so unless there was something obvious that he had failed to see then Wyman, in all of this, was still the common denominator. From Richard's point of view the plot had thickened with the only common thread being Mr Wyman.

If only life was so simple.

Chapter 10

The dice had been cast. Having met with Fionnuala and Danny there was only one more thing to do and that was the short drive to Eamonn's bungalow up in Louth. He would be the last person to visit before returning home to Kent, but in essence it could turn out to be the most dangerous part of his trip, for County Louth was known to be quite a stronghold for the IRA and those that empathise with their philosophy.

God Jean would not be very pleased at his decision to do these minor detours especially as he'd promised to go back to Kent. Still it was only for a couple of hours then he was heading home. He felt he definitely needed to meet with Eamonn if only to check out Seamus. Also he still wasn't too sure of Jimmy.

He parked his car well away from Eamonn's place to avoid causing him any embarrassment and set off to walk the relatively short distance to his bungalow on the outskirts of the town. As he walked along the road he sensed rather than saw curtains twitch, he felt a thousand invisible eyes boring into him and yet the place seemed deserted.

It took him about ten minutes to cover the short distance from his car to Eamonn's front door yet it seemed like a lifetime. Not once did he falter, or look to either side. Not once did he check behind – albeit he was sorely tempted to do so for he knew this area for what it was, and it didn't pay to look around too much. Richard strode purposely up to the front door and gave it a resounding knock then waited for the 'goon' to open it, but he got a welcome surprise. Eamonn no longer had the 'goon' there, but he had as his replacement the 'old boy' that had been in charge of the IRA patrol at the 'Holiday Camp', and he immediately recognised Richard.

"Ah b'jesus look who we have here. If it isn't Mr O'Shea's old friend…"

"Who is it?" Eamonn's voice echoed eerily in the passageway as he called to the old man from his room.

"T'is the Englishman t'at was working at the Holiday Camp, you know Kelly and Patrick's place," he called back to Eamonn.

"Y'er mean Richard, is that who yer mean?"

"T' be sure it is Richard Eamonn."

"Then bring him in man, bring him in."

The old man ushered Richard into the back room where Eamonn was busy poring over some papers, but as Richard entered he shuffled them into a pile and pushed them to one side.

"Hello Richard. 'T is good to see you. I heard you haven't been too well of late." Richard gave a wry smile.

"Hmm. What you've heard Eamonn is a slight exaggeration." Eamonn looked intrigued. "Are you suggesting things are not what they seem?"

"Something along those lines, but it's a long story."

"Well I've got plenty of time."

"I'm sure you have Eamonn, but it will have to wait." At this juncture Eamonn summoned the 'old boy' and presented him with a list of items.

"Here you are, take this and the car and go into Louth and get these things. Also you best check on the lads. Make sure that everything's OK and bring me their weekly reports. Don't rush back I've got some business to discuss with our friend here."

With that the 'old boy' took the hint and armed with the list, the car keys and some money he departed. Eamonn followed him to the front door and just to make sure that they would not be disturbed he locked it.

"Do you fancy a drop of Bushmills?"

"No thanks Eamonn. I'm only passing through and I've got a fair drive ahead of me."

Same old Eamonn just a bit older but aren't we all.

"Now Richard what's this all about?" Eamonn asked in a business like way.

"I wondered if you could give me some information, that's all."

"What sort of information?" Initially the talk was about old times, the 'Holiday Camp', Kelly and Pat. About Breandán O'Shea and the trials and tribulations of those early days and how Richard had eventually joined the 'circus' and how he lost his men in Louth. Slowly but surely Richard skilfully manipulated the conversation around to the attack on 'slab' Riley's farm, of how it failed and how Bobby Racain had ended up being killed because of poor intelligence.

"What do you mean poor intelligence?"

"Well nobody advised us about the back-up power supplies did they, so we unwittingly walked into a trap, right up to our necks in the shit so to speak." Eamonn's brow furrowed.

"Surely you were told by Lisburn?"

"Not a bloody word. When I queried it they said no information had been passed to them by intelligence. Anyway weren't you part of the intelligence?"

"Yes and so was Danny and Wyman."

Here we go again, my friend Wyman! I wonder who was responsible for obtaining the intelligence on the back-up generators etc. I bet it was Wyman.

"So what went wrong Eamonn, why weren't we told about the generators?"

"As far as I knew Lisburn was informed. I told Wyman what I knew, but it was down to him in the end."

Just as I thought, Wyman again. This is too much of a coincidence!

"You say it was Wyman's responsibility."

"Yes, but I know it was passed up the line. I saw his report."
Hmm, I'm not so sure.

Richard continued to question Eamonn about the failed Riley operation trying all the time to figure out where the problem occurred. From what Eamonn said it didn't conclusively show that Wyman was the culprit. According to Eamonn Wyman had done his groundwork, in fact they all had and the intelligence was sound and had been passed up the line.

"So where is Wyman now?"

"Last I heard he had been pulled out from here and was back in London. The bush telegraph says that he got a posting overseas – Libya or somewhere, but I can't confirm that."

Well where do I go from here then?

"Thanks Eamonn, you've been a great help." Richard glanced at his watch. "Shit is that the time, I'd better get going." He stood up as if to go then as an afterthought asked one more question. "What about a guy called Seamus – does that name mean anything to you?"

"Seamus? Seamus?" Eamonn looked thoughtful for a moment or two then shook his head, "I can't say that it does, apart from what I heard on the grapevine."

"And what was that?"

"Oh just that a guy called Seamus was instrumental with another operator in the bombing of Dublin, but he was handled either by Dublin or some woman in the South – Swords I think it was. Yes Swords, definitely Swords. Why, should it mean something to me?"

If what you say is true Eamonn then that would explain a lot, it would point to Rosie being his handler and he would have thought I was instrumental in her demise. Shit!

"Not unless you were his handler. It's just that it was suggested that he was possibly being handled by someone north of Dublin that's all. By the way were you ever handled by Wyman?"

"Yes, but a long time ago. Why do you ask? What's the great interest in Wyman?"

Wouldn't you like to know!

"Nothing really just trying to fathom out a few things. Anyway thanks again Eamonn." He unlocked the front door and shook Richard's hand then watched him as he walked back along the road.

Now I wonder what all that was about Mr James. I think I need to watch out for you.

As Richard started the car's engine he mulled over the conversation he had had with both Danny and Eamonn, especially the bit about Seamus. Danny had suggested that there was a distinct possibility that Eamonn had been the handler for Seamus and yet he denied all knowledge of him. Eamonn had been handled by Wyman, so had Danny as well as Austen. Rosie had been eliminated and she had been the handler for Seamus, or so it seemed. Richard felt he now had a need to get back to Kent and to subsequently meet with Sir James. There certainly appeared to be a pattern emerging. As to Seamus he didn't know the answer.

Chapter 11

The letterbox rattled announcing the arrival of the post and a single postcard of Portrush fluttered to the floor. Portrush is a lovely seaside town and being built on a peninsular it can boast of not one but two exceptional beaches and of course some of the most wonderful panoramic views across to Donegal, Dunluce Castle and the Giant's Causeway headland. However, like many Irish towns, there is a darker historical side to Portrush, for it is believed that it was here that in 1103 whilst engaged in one of the most bloody of battles with Irish forces, Magnus Barefoot, King of Norway was killed and his army routed by the Irish. Richard picked up the postcard and read the brief message.

> *Having a lovely holiday. Jimmy eventually agreed to*
> *the break so now enjoying the sea air. We've found*
> *some interesting samples for you. Back home next week*
> *will see you then.*
> *Love Angie*

With eyes half closed he stared at the card as if deep in thought, then smiled.

OK Jean so you weren't joking when you said you would send me a postcard, but what does it mean?

He read and re-read the cryptic message trying to think behind the words, trying to think like Jean. He dug deep into the recesses of his mind, going back to basics on passing simple messages.

What was it they had said in training? Keep a message brief, innocent looking, but choose your words carefully. Use wording that can be linked to the project being undertaken. In your message give an innocent clue!

He looked at the message again and thought back to just over a week ago.

Now what was it Jean had said?

"Yes of course. That's what it was."

He suddenly realized he had spoken out loud and the sitting room door was open. A quick check confirmed no harm was done as Anne, his wife, was nowhere to be seen. What had got him so excited was the fact that he distinctly remembered Jean saying that Sean had logged some information somewhere which could probably help, but at the time she did not know where he had put the document or papers. According to the postcard she had got Jimmy on board, appeared to have found the elusive papers and wanted a meeting at her house next week. This recent development was certainly moving things in the right direction, but before he could even contemplate returning to Ireland there were plans to be made and equipment to be obtained. He was now thinking like the Richard of old. He was not going to leave anything to chance.

The day had a definite autumnal feel to it. You could smell the change in the air, the light breeze had a chill to it and birds such as the swifts and the swallows had already migrated, flying south on the first stage of their long flight to Africa and a warmer climate. Even though there was a chill to the breeze it was still relatively mild for the time of year, after all it was October and winter was just around the corner. Richard made his way into the Hilton foyer to his pre-arranged meeting with Sir James. He glanced at his watch; it said 12:50, he was ten minutes early.

Better to be ten minutes early than five minutes late.

He spotted an unoccupied leather settee at the far end of the lobby and immediately made his way over to it. He did not have to wait too long before he spotted the tall distinguished figure of Sir James heading his way.

"Richard, good to see you," he said holding out his hand.

"And you Sir James." Richard stood up and shook the hand of Sir James.

"Come dear boy; let us find a quiet corner in the cocktail bar. That is of course if such a thing exists at this time of day." With that Sir James about-turned and with Richard in close pursuit he set off in the direction of the cocktail bar.

Having organised some drinks and having found the elusive quiet corner Sir James was now happy to listen to Richard.

"Well Richard, you said it was urgent that we meet, so here I am, fire away."

"Well, it's like this Sir James. About ten days ago I went over to Ireland – on my own – with a view to seeing what if anything I could uncover over there. The main reason was to see a couple of my ex-colleagues who I trust socially as well as professionally…"

"What about Paul?"

"I left Paul back here checking out certain things in and around Kent."

I am sorry Sir James but I'm not telling you every last detail, well not yet anyway.

"Anyway, as I was saying, I went over to Ireland to meet with an old contact near Dublin, but I managed to pick up a tail so to speak. Now I don't know how they knew I was over there, but they certainly did that's for sure, and what's more they now know my car. Oh and just to put you further in the picture, my contact was, shall we say taken out of the frame. Pity really because she was a good operator, one of the best I would say. So Sir James I will be returning to Ireland in the very near future but before I do there are a few things I need."

"Fire away and I'll see what can be done."

"I need a clean car, one that cannot be traced and certainly one that will not stand out in a crowd. It needs to be a wolf in sheep's clothing. Not your average bog standard engine, but one that moves rapidly, a Ford or similar with a 'breathed on' engine would be ideal. In addition to the car…"

"Whoa, hold on Richard I need to make a note of this otherwise I'll forget something."
Sir James pulled a small notebook and a pen from his inside pocket and started to take down Richard's shopping list.

"So is that the lot?"

"I think so Sir James."

"Listen, this is what I've got – Ford car, up-rated engine, but standard looking." He glanced up at Richard. Richard nodded. "Secure radio with special frequency allocation linked directly to my office." Again he gave Richard a fleeting look, for a second time the nod of acknowledgement. "Electronic gizmos all sorts of devices, tracking devices, GPS device, bugs and telephone bugs etc., etc."

"That's about it Sir James," Richard said, then as an afterthought, "there is one thing more Sir James - I need a weapon. A 9.00mm would be useful, one that cannot be traced." Sir James pulled a face.

"That may prove a little difficult, but I'm sure it can be done. So Richard you need these by when?"

"Day after tomorrow."

"What!" he exclaimed, "the day after tomorrow?"

"Yes, I'm serious Sir James." Sir James pursed his lips and gave a low whistle.

"That certainly is a tall order."

"I know it is, but if I am to be effective then I need those things." Sir James sat back in his chair and with eyes half closed he stared at some imaginary spot on the ceiling whilst he mulled over Richard's request. Suddenly he opened his eyes, sat up in his chair and looked straight at Richard. His mind was made up.

"OK. If that's what it takes then so be it you'll have everything you've asked for ready for you in 48 hours."

"There is one last thing Sir James," Sir James raised a quizzical eyebrow. "From now on I've decided to call this operation by the codename *Beggarman*."

"As in *Rich-man, Poor-man, Beggarman Thief?*" Sir James enquired.

"That's right Sir James, so if you wouldn't mind, refer to me by the codename *Beggarman* and I think for you..." he paused and a slight smile flitted across his face, "perhaps *Rich-man* would be quite appropriate." The irony wasn't lost on Sir James.

"I see, so that's how you see me Mr James...OK I get the picture," he answered. "So I'm *Rich-man* and you're *Beggarman*. Hmm, well at least my name isn't *Thief* so I suppose I should count my blessings. So who is *Thief?*"

"Ah that name I reserved for the mole. You see Sir James no matter which way you look at it a 'mole' in my book ios a traitor and a thief so I think it is quite appropriate to codename him or her as such." Sir James nodded his approval. "So may I suggest that from now on we use the codenames at all times – apart from when we are face to face that is – and it is especially important when we communicate with each other by radio just in case we are overheard...I'm sure you understand." Sir James nodded in agreement.

The plates on the car deck reverberated as the engines were placed in full reverse. The rope around the ferry's capstan tightened almost to breaking point as the full thrust of the engines pulled the ferry astern. A fine spray of water flicked from the ever tightening rope as it creaked and groaned under pressure, but slowly, ever so slowly the ferry inched closer and closer to the dock side. There was a dull thud as the side of the boat made contact with the dockside. Deckhands worked quickly making sure that the ropes being wound around the capstan were coiled and stowed safely. Staccato orders were being shouted from man to man as the ferry was made fast alongside. The noise from the ship's engines died away and the turbulent foaming water being pushed passed the side of the ship by its twin propellers slowly subsided. Foot passengers had already gathered on deck waiting for the ramps that would soon become the bridges between ferry and dockside to be lowered.

Drivers made their way below passing by the open steel door to the ship's engine room where the smell of hot oil and diesel hung heavy in the air. The violent vibration and the noise of the ship's engines had now subsided only to be replaced by the sound of a multitude of car engines being started. A blue haze of exhaust fumes hung motionless on the car deck as engines were revved impatiently, drivers eager to disembark. Slowly the first of the vehicles started to move forward up the ramp and out on to the road leading from the docks and onward into Dublin. It was soon the turn of the white Ford Mondeo. Richard edged the car forward convinced that this time he would not pick up Danny or, for that matter, any other tail as he started his journey towards the border and on to Lisburn.

Chapter 12

It was late afternoon when a white Ford Mondeo turned off the main Lisburn road, and proceeded along a narrow country lane that meandered its way between the dry stone walls enclosing fields and small wooded areas. It was not long before the lane straightened, and the grazing land on the right gave way to a handful of large detached houses forming a small yet prosperous residential area on the outskirts of Lisburn. The last residence on the right was one of the biggest and boasted a large double garage, big enough to house at least three medium sized cars. It was here that Jean O'Donald lived.

As the Mondeo approached the entrance to this property it slowed to a walking pace, the driver paying particular attention to the two vehicles, a new BMW and a black Audi, which were parked side by side in front of the double garage. Instead of turning into the driveway Richard drove by the entrance and continued along the lane until he came to a narrow farm track that disappeared into the woodland off to his left. Making sure that there were no other vehicles about, he reversed his car up the track far enough to be out of sight of any passer-by who might be taking a casual stroll, or from any approaching traffic. From the glove compartment he took out what looked to be a small leather wallet and from this he removed a small disc, the back of which he slid open to reveal a tiny battery with a red tag protruding from one side. The disc was a small transmitter that when switched on would transmit a high frequency tone so acting as a positioning beacon or tracking device. Richard now removed the small red plastic tag, which had served as a crude form of switch by isolating the transmitter's circuitry from its power source, and slid the battery compartment closed. The device was now armed and fully functional.

On the back seat of the car lay a small lockable black leather case not unlike the type of briefcase used by thousands of white collar workers, but that was as far as the similarities went. Unlike its counterpart, this case did not carry documents but instead it housed the sophisticated electronic circuitry needed to track a 'would-be' target via military satellites. Richard opened the case to reveal a small screen with three or four pushbuttons and switches situated below. He pushed the button labelled on/off and the screen sprang to life with a series of what appeared to be town names all jumbled together, these gradually cleared and a map of Northern Ireland came up on the screen. At the top of the display a small menu appeared asking for town name, address, postcode and route to be input plus a Personal Identification Number or PIN. Richard input the name Lisburn followed by his PIN. Almost straight away a satellite view of Lisburn appeared. Next he was asked to wait whilst the Global Positioning System located the satellites for it to perform various calculations and within thirty seconds he had displayed in front of him a detailed map of the locality he was in, even down to Jean O'Donald's house. On the display were two blips one right in the centre flashing green for his base station – the Mondeo, the other slightly overlapping and flashing red - the small transmitter he held in his hand.

Leaving the case where it was, Richard locked the door of the Mondeo and walked along the track to a point where once more the woodland gave way to pasture land. Here he secreted the transmitter in the long grass at the base of the dry stone wall noting that it was the tenth stone along from the field gate post. He then returned to the car where he checked that the signal was being detected by his receiver in the attaché case. Sure enough the red blip was showing – according to the map it was to the rear of the car and off to his left approximately two to three hundred yards away. Having satisfied himself that his base tracking station worked, he now needed to reassure himself that a small handheld version worked equally well. From the glove compartment he extracted what appeared to be a small handheld transceiver, but again that was as far as the resemblance went. Like its larger counterpart it had a small display housed beneath a flip cover where it replicated in miniature exactly what was being displayed on the main base station. Again the base station appeared as a green blip with the target as a red blip. Armed with the portable version he once again set off along the track checking from time to time that the red blip was still visible. With the aid of the portable global positioning system Richard took no time at all to locate the concealed transmitter.

Good. Now let's see whose side you're batting for Jimmy?
All he had to do now to keep tabs on Jimmy was to attach the transmitter to the Audi.

Cautiously he edged forward, pressing his body hard up against the wall as he did so, to minimise the risk of being seen from the house. He had easily scaled the outside wall and dropped down into the corner near the garage, but now came the tricky bit. For ten feet or so he would be in view of anyone casually looking out of the windows towards the garage, but there was nothing he could do other than to duck down low and travel fast to the BMW where he would once again be shielded from view. Hopefully by doing this he would avoid discovery. With a sharp intake of breath, he bent double and ran like the wind.

Please don't be looking out of the front view window my way, well not for the next ten minutes!
In next to no time he had covered the short distance to the BMW, the first of the two cars, where he paused and steadied his breathing. Slowly and carefully he raised his head to take stock of the situation and he could just about see enough to

confirm that those inside were still blissfully unaware of his presence.

Hmm, now if I keep low around the front of Jean's car I should be out of sight, but will the Audi shield me from their view once I'm clear of the BMW?

Still keeping a low profile, Richard eased himself round the front of the BMW and carefully checked his line to the Audi. Once more he slowly edged forward, craning his neck to check on the house as he did so, but the windows were no longer in his line of sight.

OK, he thought to himself, *if I can't see them then they probably can't see me so Richard stay low and hopefully you should be hidden from view.*

One more check from where he crouched confirmed that no matter what he did he definitely could not get a line of sight to the front door or the windows.

I reckon that they won't be able to see me until I'm at least six or seven feet from the BMW and by then I should be shielded by the Audi.

Another quick look, a sharp intake of breath and within a few seconds he was bent double and racing toward the Audi. At the very last moment and with cat-like agility he sprang towards the Audi. In one fluid motion he landed, rolled into the prone position and with outstretched arm he affixed the disc to the underside of the car.

Not bad for someone out of practice!

He had covered the six or seven feet where he could have been spotted fixed the small transmitter and got back to the BMW in less than thirty seconds. All he had to do now was to retrace his footsteps from the BMW!

Ten minutes later a white Mondeo swung into the driveway and parked alongside the new BMW and the Audi. Richard James grabbed his case off the back seat of the car and nonchalantly walked up to the front door of the house. The second part of his plan was going to be a little more difficult. Because of his reservations about Jimmy, he now needed to place 'bugs' in Jean's lounge, hall and other parts of the house so he was aware of any conversations that may take place.

Perhaps Jean will invite me to stay the night now that would be helpful!

"Richard. Come in, come in." Jean ushered him into a spacious hallway and gave him a hug and a kiss on the cheek. "Lovely to see you again. Here let me take your things. I assume you'll be stopping, well at least tonight anyway."

I love it when a plan comes together.

"Well if you're sure that's no trouble, then I'd love to."

"Of course it's no trouble. Come on through, Jimmy's here."

I know he is Jean; I've just bugged his car.

"Jimmy, Richard's here," she called to Jimmy in the lounge. "Come on Richard, come through. Can I get you a drink of something, a Bushmills may be?" He smiled and nodded.

"You bet. Thanks Jean. How are you Jimmy, long time no see."

"I'm fine Richard. How's life been treating you since your retirement from the 'circus'?" He flashed a welcoming smile.

Huh, retirement my arse. If you do work for Sir James then you would know that I was stitched up, so come on Jimmy give me some credit.

"I'm getting by, you know, doing a bit of this and a bit of that. So what are you doing with yourself nowadays?"

"I think you know the answer to that one Richard, don't you?"

Of course I do.

"You're right, just as you know what I'm doing, so why don't we stop the fencing and get down to business?"

"Touché Richard, touché. OK, Jean told me you need our help but as you know, I wasn't too keen on the idea. Anyway, she's persuaded me for old time's sake to do whatever I can, so where do we go with this?"

That depends on you my friend and what I find out over the next few days about you. Can I really trust you again?

"I believe Jean told you that I feel sure that it was somebody high up in the 'circus' that set me up and as such I'm desperate to... how shall I say...to get some leads."

"Then what?"

"Well may be then I can move forward and start living once again. I do believe you and Jean have discovered some information for me."

"It's more a case of Jean than me. I will of course do whatever I can old friend...but that may not amount to much."

"One Bushmills for a dear friend. Here Jimmy lets have a toast...to old friends. I give you Richard."

"Yes, to old friends and especially to you Richard. Cheers."

All three raised their glasses in a toast to their old friendship.

"Cheers Jimmy and Jean."

With the evening meal out of the way and with Jimmy agreeing to help, the three of them sat down to look at the 'samples', as Jean had previously called them. Laid out on the table in front of them were diaries that her late husband Sean had kept, in which he had meticulously logged things that he felt were relevant and of some major importance in his line of work as a member of the UDR 'circus'. He had kept the diaries purely as some form of insurance and had lodged them with a solicitor as he did not trust anyone, because in his position he could not afford the luxury of 'trust'. He was certain that during the 1970s and 1980s that many good operators had been lost to the enemy because they trusted the wrong person and that someone, somewhere in the 'circus' had betrayed them. Sean had a feeling that somebody high up in the 'circus' was betraying them. He was convinced that there was a 'mole' or a double agent in their midst but he could never prove it. That was until one day he stumbled on some information that was to ultimately cost him his life!

"Here Richard this is interesting." Jean pointed to an entry in the 1975 diary. "Look it says here that O'Rourke studied International Politics at Magee College back in the 1960s."

"But there's nothing unusual in that."

"Of course not, unless you just happen to be friends with someone who has strong links with the Officials, the OIRA."

"Who was that Jean?" asked Jimmy.

"James O'Shea."

"How do you know he was great friends with him?"

"Because James O'Shea studied medicine at Magee College."

"T' be sure he did, but that doesn't make them great friends," scoffed Jimmy. "Just because they are both at the same university doesn't necessarily make them friends. A university is a big establishment; they probably didn't even know each other…"

"You may say that Jimmy, but look here…" Richard pointed to another entry at a later date, "it states here that Sean actually managed to track down an old girlfriend of O'Rourke's, and that she said that they were friends to the point that when O'Rourke got into financial difficulties O'Shea bailed him out. Now that for my money ties them together as pretty close friends."

"Does it give the girl's name, or anything about her?" *If we had her name we could possibly trace her and may be that would help.*

"Nah, nothing's that simple Jimmy."

"Hang on Richard I'm sure I've seen something in the diaries about a girlfriend of O'Rourke." Jean hastily started to flick over the pages of the different diaries spread out on the table. "Yes, I knew it." She gave a jubilant cry. "There, it's Mary, Mary White."

All three of them peered simultaneously at the entry which read: -

August 15th 1981 – tracked down Mary White girlfriend of O. Found her living in flat in Derry. Spoke to her she confirms O'Rourke was her boyfriend whilst at Magee – she also studied Politics. He was great friends with O'Shea who loaned him some money when he got into difficulties. O was target for IRA recruitment. James O'Shea introduced him to his older brother Breandán.

"Well, well, well." Jimmy gave a low whistle. "So our Major O'Rourke was courted by the Officials."

"But I still don't see it," said Jean. "If he was recruited into the IRA then how come Intelligence never knew?"

"Either he was never recruited or he has been very clever what do you reckon Jimmy?"

"B'jesus this is dynamite and I t'ink we certainly need further proof. We need to check out the fine detail and go through these diaries, and any other documents you've got Jean, with a fine tooth comb, because this could prove to be one helluva hot potato!"

After three hours of checking and re-checking the diary entries they were about to give up when Richard accidentally knocked a pile of them onto the floor. As he reached down to pick them up, a folded sheet of paper fell from one and gently fluttered down to settle at his feet. Richard bent down to retrieve the folded sheet but as he did so a photograph of a woman in her mid thirties taken outside a pub, spilled onto the floor face up. Realising that the photograph was not a photograph of Jean he hastily covered it with his foot. Fortunately for Richard, both Jimmy and Jean were so engrossed in looking for information they did not notice him bend down and retrieve the folded sheet of paper and the photograph. He gave a cursory look in Jean's direction, and then glanced towards Jimmy just to reassure himself that they were fully engaged in what they were doing before he casually opened the folded sheet and glanced at the contents. The first thing he noticed was the name Ryan Lamar as it jumped out at him from the paper he held in his hand.

What has Ryan Lamar got in common with O'Rourke?
Richard quickly scanned the page he held in his hand and it wasn't long before he realised that what he was looking at was damning evidence that O'Rourke was somehow mixed up with Lamar, who in turn was linked to Imanos. This latter situation had already been confirmed by Johnny Rains. Where had he seen Lamar's name written before?

Of course, Lamar's name had been on the sheet of paper at the farm used by Seamus.
Richard thought back to the farm and pictured the sheet of paper recalling what he had seen written there.

His name was also on the Social Network Diagram that Seamus had drawn, but O'Rourke's wasn't.
He pictured the Social Network Diagram in his mind's eye.

Seamus had drawn a link to a question mark in the box labelled UK and an indirect link between MI6 and the question mark, which would mean Lamar, was indirectly linked to MI6. If the question mark is the mole is it O'Rourke, is he Thief or is it someone else, Wyman or even Ash? Had Seamus in fact taken up where Sean had left off, or was it pure coincidence?
Richard carefully folded the piece of paper up and slipped it into his pocket.

"Richard, here is another entry reference to O'Rourke's time at Magee." Jimmy pointed to an entry which stated that 'O' – presumably O'Rourke – had socialist leanings and whilst at Magee appeared to actively promote the views and sympathies of the Irish Republican Socialist Party, the IRSP for short.

"It certainly looks as if our Major has some explaining to do!"

"That may well be true Jimmy, but it still doesn't prove a thing." He paused in thought for a moment then went on, "Jimmy, have you ever heard of a bloke called Lamar, Ryan Lamar?" Jimmy thought about it for a while then shook his head.

"Not particularly, heard a few rumours but that's all, why?"

"Well Lamar, Ryan Lamar to give him his full name, was around in Kent and appeared to be friends with a guy called Imanos. Imanos was one of the blokes involved in the snatch squad that Paul and I were training ready for 'Operation Orpheus'. Now I think Lamar may well have a lot to do with O'Rourke along with the failure of 'Operation Orpheus' and my downfall. I think that if I can find out where he fits in with all this then I'll be able to clear my name."

"I don't see that Richard, because Wyman..." Jimmy started to say before being cut short by Richard.

"I don't think so. Wyman is a red herring..." but Jimmy interrupted him.

"How can you say that? Wyman was Austen's handler – he got arrested. Wyman is the intelligence with reference to power and communications supplied to Riley's place – you get bad intelligence - operation is catastrophic..."

"Yes agreed," Richard said cutting Jimmy off in mid-sentence, "but Wyman rescued us and brought us home. He took me to a safe house..."

"And you were attacked...come on Richard just think about it Wyman crops up time and time again, especially when things go tits up, he must be..."But before Jimmy could complete what he was about to say Richard tossed the sheet of paper that he found onto the table.

"If you don't believe me then look at what Sean has written on there." Jimmy picked up the paper that Richard had tossed, with some annoyance, onto the table and read out aloud what Sean had written:

'Mary White confirms that O'Rourke great friends with the O'Shea family, James O'Shea bailed him out of financial difficulty. He joined the IRSP when he was introduced to Ryan Lamar an IRSP activist. A young man called Wyman came on the scene and befriended O'Rourke back in the 60s; he was very friendly at one time she thought he was something to do with the IRSP but she eventually found out he was not. O'Rourke joined British Army – intelligence she thought, would tell me more tomorrow. Met with her following day, seemed afraid no mention of O'Rourke, said I would return next day. Note: my contact eliminated – no body IRA?
26th August 1983
Filed report on 'slab' Riley. Gave details to control about Riley being major player in Northern Command Provisionals. Need to eliminate him, his farm straddles the border it is a high security unit with many personnel. Has back-up generators on power so will need to consider these prior to any possible attack. Riley instrumental in extortion, murder and many bombings. This info has been filed as a report with control.'

His eyes stared at the sheet of paper in his hand and a hushed silence descended on the small group gathered there. Richard was the first to speak.

"Jean, that date, isn't it the day before Sean's death?" he asked.

"Yes it is," she replied somewhat sombrely.

"Interesting…"*O'Rourke was in charge over here at that time. I wonder…* "I think it is patently obvious that O'Rourke is a problem…no not a problem worse than that… a danger to the department. What do you think Jimmy?"

"I'm not sure. May be a visit to Wyman might shed some light on things."

153

"No, that's too risky. I know according to Sean's notes and his contacts it looks as if Wyman recruited O'Rourke into the 'circus' but regardless of what I said earlier I still think we ought to give Wyman a wide berth for now."

"So you agree Wyman is the problem," Jimmy retorted.

"I didn't say that. What I did say was that we give him a wide berth…let's just eliminate him…"

"How do you mean eliminate him?" asked Jean a little concerned.

"Not like that Jean, I don't mean kill him, I mean eliminate him as a suspect before we go charging in."

"Good,' she looked relieved. "I'm pleased you clarified that. For a moment there you had me worried."

"So what do you propose we do?" asked Jimmy.

"For starters Jimmy your codename will be *Poor-man* and I need you to check out Wyman's pedigree. Find out anything and everything about the man. Go back to the time he was supposed to have befriended O'Rourke…what he was doing…what his position was within the 'circus'…and of course any friends he had at the time."

"OK Richard. Anything else?"

"Hmm, the girl…"

"What girl?"

"O'Rourke's girlfriend, see what you can find out about her." Richard tossed him the photograph of Mary White. "Here, get some copies of that done and let Jean and I have one. Incidentally have you ever seen that photograph before Jean?" Jimmy passed the photograph of the girl to Jean, who looked long and hard at the head and shoulder shot of the thirty something and shook her head.

"No, never. Where did you get that from Richard?"

"It was inside that folded sheet of paper," he said indicating the sheet of paper which now lay on the table in front of Jimmy. Jean looked back at the face of the girl and racked her brains, but she couldn't place her. She turned the photograph over to see if there was anything written on the back – all it said was Bogside Inn 1983, which was in Derry.

What was Sean doing in Derry he never operated there and even if he did the Bogside area was definitely no-go for a Protestant, unless he was undercover?

"Have you seen this?" She passed the photograph to Jimmy so he could read the back. He pursed his lips and gave a low whistle.

"Perhaps someone knew about this and that was why Sean was killed."

"Knew about what Jimmy?" asked Richard.

"This…" Jimmy passed him the upturned photograph so that he could also read what was written on the back.

"Hmm, 1983…was Sean undercover ops at that time Jean?"

"I'm not sure. He could have been. I rarely knew what he did. You must be able to find that out Jimmy." Jimmy nodded his head.

"Yeah I suppose I could but is it really important? I think we must assume that he was undercover and that this woman was one of his contacts. If that's the case then Mary White is a codename." Once again a momentary silence ensued. "Anyway unless there is anything else, I'm going to make a move," Jimmy said as he pushed back the chair he was sitting on and stood up to go.

"No I think we've covered everything we can, don't you Jean?" asked Richard.

"T' be sure we have. Would you like a drink of something before you go Jimmy?" Jean asked.

"No thanks Jean, I must get off now." He turned to Richard and extended his hand. "Good to see you again Richard."

"And you too Jimmy take care now."

"Sure I will and you too. I'll be in touch as soon as I have something. Goodnight to the both of yer."

"Be careful Jimmy because you never know who is watching you!" Richard smiled, safe in the knowledge that he could keep an eye on Jimmy's movements all right.

Yes my friend be very careful because I'm watching you and while you're busy doing your checks I'll run some checks on you because the jury is still out as far as you're concerned!

Chapter 13

The Bogside was a powder keg, a no-go area for those of the Protestant persuasion. It was known the world over – not for its culture, not for its charm not even for the poverty that some of the inhabitants obviously still lived in, but for its violence. The bombings, the barricades, the hail of rubber bullets, the armed men in black ski masks and balaclavas, the Provisional Irish Republican Army (PIRA for short)! Where Rossville Street meets Fahan Street one finds the wall known as 'Free Derry Corner'. In 1969, John 'Caker' Casey a local inhabitant painted the wall with the words 'You are now entering Free Derry.' But that was some years ago and a lot of water had flowed under the bridge since then.

The sky was dull and overcast and there was a hint of drizzle in the air as the man shuffled aimlessly along the pavement towards the Bogside Inn. On his head he wore a peaked cap pulled down over his eyes and from the corner of his mouth dangled the remains of a hand rolled cigarette. His hands, blue with cold, were thrust deeply into the pockets of the dark blue threadbare jacket which he wore buttoned up to his chin. The collar of the jacket was turned up in a vain attempt to keep out the wind and rain. He wore a pair of grey baggy trousers and on his feet an old pair of boots. His face had a couple of day's growth of beard so adding to the illusion of poverty. Had anyone been able to see his bloodshot eyes they would have been forgiven for thinking that this man was down on his luck, a very poor man. In fact if they had taken the trouble to look closely at his eyes the local IRA soldiers would have soon realized that this man showed no fear. His eyes piercing and blue were ice cold. He took no prisoners. Although he was *Poor-man* today, he was known by many different names and had years of experience behind him. He shuffled his way along the path to the door of the Bogside Inn and pushed it ajar. He was immediately greeted by the chink of glasses and the sound of male voices. The smell of stale beer and tobacco smoke pervaded his nostrils and the strains of 'Only Our Rivers Run Free' a Republican song percolated through the chatter. As the door opened wider all conversation ceased. The clientele stared at the stranger as he shuffled his way into the bar and all that could be heard were the lyrics:

> *I drink to the death of her manhood,*
> *Those men who would rather have died*
> *Than to live in the cold chains of bondage,*
> *To bring back their rights were denied.*
> *Oh where are you now when we need you,*
> *What burns where the flame used to be,*
> *Are ye gone like the snows of last winter,*
> *And will only our rivers run free.*

"Huh and what would yer be wanting?" the barman asked the stranger eyeing him up and down suspiciously.

"I'll have a pint of bitter," the stranger replied.

"I've not seen yer before. Are yer from Derry?"

"Huh," the stranger grunted. "Just arrived and I'm looking for some digs. A mate of moin told me his sister lived out this side of t'city. I t'ink she's called Bernadette." The barman looked thoughtful for a moment then shook his head.

"What's she look like?"

"In her late thirties early forties, I've a picture in my pocket." The stranger tossed a dog-eared photograph of a woman on the bar. "There, that's her." He picked up his pint and took a mouthful. The barman studied the photograph for a little while before returning it to the stranger.

"I'm not sure; I may know her. If it's who I t'ink it is she will be here just gone six, that's after she's finished work. Who shall I say was asking for her?"

"Don't worry; I'll be back at six." With that the stranger picked up his pint, nodded his thanks and shuffled over to a table near the door where he sat apparently absorbed in rubbing his hands together to get the circulation going. The locals soon lost interest in the stranger and the chink of glasses and conversation soon returned to normal.

So it appears as if my contact was right. Bernadette alias Mary White still seems to be very much alive and kicking. Perhaps she got scared off by someone, I wonder who?

The locals in the Bogside Inn may not have shown much interest in the stranger but someone not too far away was very interested in what he was up to.

A white Mondeo slowly cruised along Duke Street the driver obviously looking for a particular house number, apparently he did not find the house because at the end he stopped and parked. He opened a black attaché case as if to check on the correct address. He surreptitiously lifted a sheaf of papers to one side as they were concealing a small GPS screen. He pushed the on/off switch and his action almost immediately brought the screen to life. A map of the area filled the screen. A green blinking circle of light at the bottom of Duke Street indicated where he was. A solid red circle of light appeared in what looked to be a public house called the Bogside Inn.

So why are you there Jimmy my old mate?

There was a tap on the window and Richard looked up at a young lad's face pressed against the nearside front window. As soon as the lad saw him looking he stuck out his tongue then ran away, then from a safe distance he started to throw stones at the car.

Time to move Richard, the last thing you need is to attract attention.

With that he shut the case lid, put the car into gear and moved off. As he passed the young lad he heard him shouting various obscenities as he pelted stones at the back of the car. In a short space of time he was clear of the Bogside and rapidly heading for the Protestant area of the city.

The Fountain Estate in Londonderry is bordered by Bishop Street, Upper Bennett Street, Abercorn Road and Hawkin Street and is a Loyalist stronghold in what is predominately a Catholic area to the city and mirrors its counterpart over in the Waterside area of Londonderry. On the Fountain Estate, like Waterside, not only will the visitor find many Loyalist murals depicting the Red Hand of Ulster and Union Jacks which reflect its truly Unionist tradition, they will also bear witness to the armed patrols of the Protestant paramilitary forces of which the main contingency is that of the Ulster Defence Association (UDA). The houses, like the inhabitants, were battle-scarred and weary, in fact the whole estate could have done with a makeover. It was in this Protestant stronghold that Richard eventually stopped. He desperately needed to put in a call on his secure radio link to Sir James to advise him of his progress, but more to the point he wanted a full screening check to be carried out on Seamus, Wyman and of course Jimmy. It didn't take long for him to contact Sir James and update him on his progress. Sir James listened patiently to what Richard had to say and noted his request for the screening to be carried out before replying.

"You say you want screening to be carried out on Wyman, Seamus and Jimmy?"

"That's correct *Rich-man*. Over."

I wish you would use correct radio procedure Sir James instead of expecting me to guess when you have finished speaking.

"Hmm. Jimmy you say…"

"Yes *Rich-man*, is that a problem, over."

"Well…I suppose not. Wyman fair enough and even Seamus is OK, but Jimmy works for me… and to be honest that in itself is a good recommendation, so why Jimmy, is there a problem? Err Over."

"No *Rich-man* there is no problem, it's just that I didn't realize Jimmy worked for you. In that case disregard Jimmy but if I could ask you to press ahead with the other two I would appreciate it. Over."

"Very good *Beggarman*. I suppose sooner rather than later...Hmm over."

"Roger *Rich-man*. As soon as possible, over."

"Very good. Call me tomorrow. I may have something for you then. Over."

"Thank you *Rich-man* out."

"Bye *Beggarman* out."

Dear me Sir James you made heavy weather of that.

At fifteen minutes to six a gleaming black Audi glided almost silently up to the kerbside not far from Free Derry Corner and stopped. The driver an attractive woman, well dressed, nice figure and in her late forties looked the part yet the passenger, a scruffy looking individual with a couple of day's stubble showing, and dressed in a threadbare dark blue jacket, looked out of place in such a car. All in all they made an odd couple and had there been anyone about they may well have raised an eyebrow at the obviously well-to-do lady giving a lift to such a down and out. On the other hand they may well have chuckled inwardly thinking to themselves,

What a lucky guy to meet such a kindly woman who was obviously out of his class but only too happy to give him a lift.
The man opened his door and got out pulling a rolled up cap from his pocket as he did so. Without saying a word he pulled the cap down over his eyes, acknowledged the driver with a slight wave of the hand, jammed his hands into his jacket pockets and shuffled off down the road in the direction of the

Bogside. At just before six the stranger pushed open the door of the Bogside Inn and shuffled up to the bar.

"A pint please," he asked in a gruff Belfast accent and tossed two one pound coins onto the bar.

The barman picked up the coins, rang up one pound eighty and gave the stranger twenty pence change without saying a word.

"Yer did say Bernadette comes in here didn't yer?"

"T'be sure any time now," was the surly reply.

The stranger picked up his pint and shuffled to a seat where he could keep an eye on the comings and goings as reflected in the mirror opposite the door. The positioning of the mirror was no accident; it was there to forewarn some of the less savoury individuals of any potential encounters with the British Security Forces or the Ulster Defence Regiment. At least they could make an attempt to get through to the other bar before they were seen then out through the private quarters should the need arise.

It was just after six when Bernadette entered the Bogside Inn. She was of average height, short hair with blonde highlights. She must have been mid to late thirties still with a shapely figure, perhaps she carried a little weight around her midriff, but nothing too obvious. In fact she looked good for her age dressed in tight jeans and a skimpy v-necked top that accentuated her large breasts.

"Hello Colm, I'll have gin and bitter lemon please."

"What's wrong with your usual tonight? Come into some money have yer?" Colm quipped sarcastically.

"Yer cheeky bastard just fer that yer best make it a large one."

"I'll give yer a large one all right…"

"Oi behave Colm."

"Drink I meant, not'ing else…" Colm gave her a broad grin, "What about moin then?" he asked.

"Sorry Colm, would yer be having a drink with me t'en?"

"Well, t'ank yer very much, I'll take fer it now and be having moin later."

"Yer won't Colm McShane, yer be drinking it now or not at all…"

"T'be sure yer a hard one Bernadette. I'll be having a pint t'en. T'ank yer very much t'at will be six punt twenty." She gave him a ten pound note. "Here yer are, three punt eighty change. By the way, some bloke over there is asking fer yer. I told him yer be in by six." Bernadette glanced across at the stranger with the dark blue jacket sitting over the other side of the bar. A puzzled look crossed her face, she didn't recognise him but then that was not surprising as she had never clapped eyes on him before.

"Did he say what he wanted?"

"No, just said he was a mate of yer brother and he was looking fer some digs."

"OK thanks Colm." She picked up her drink and her handbag and wiggled her way across the bar. The wiggle was really for Colm's benefit.

"Hello, I'm Bernadette. Colm said yer were looking fer me?" The stranger looked up at the woman standing before him and nodded.

"Do yer mind if I sit down?" He grunted his reply. "I'll take that as a yes, please join me." With that she pulled up a stool and sat down.

"Colm said yer were a friend of Dermot's and yer were looking fer some digs, is t'at right?"

"Yes 't'is right enough."

"Are so yer do speak t'en. My name's Bernadette, pleased t'meet yer…I didn't catch yer name."

"Probably 'cause I didn't tell yer. My name's Conánn. Pleased t'meet yer Bernadette."

Or should I really call you Mary.

"So where yer from Conánn?"

"I'm from the twenty-six counties."

"Yer do surprise me, yer accent sounds more Belfast way than anything."

"Well that's probably because I was born there, but I'm living in Wicklow, well I was. I'm up here to find some work... a coming home yer could say." Slowly Bernadette started to warm to this stranger who was a friend of her brother's. "Can yer put me up fer a couple of days until I get something more permanent?" She thought about it for a moment or two.

Well I suppose I could. After all I do have a spare room and the extra cash would always come in useful.

"OK. It will cost yer."

"How much?"

"Ten a night."

"Hmm, I'm not sure I can afford t'at...OK. So where's yer house."

"Drink up and I'll take yer there."

That's exactly what I hoped you would say.

He picked up what was left of his pint and downed it in one. Bernadette not to be outdone took two mouthfuls and her large gin and bitter lemon had also gone.

It didn't take them long to reach Bernadette's house, a mid-terrace house in Duke Street with a freshly painted red front door and matching window frames. As Bernadette fiddled with the front door lock, Conánn sensed many hidden eyes watching from behind closed curtains. In fact he was sure he had seen the curtain next door move slightly as they approached the front door, but he wasn't unduly worried. A moment later the door was open and they were inside number 40 Duke Street. The front door opened into a short hallway which gave way to a set of enclosed stairs. The hallway went on past the stairs through to a back room and a kitchen, which was the main living area. The front room, like many homes, was reserved for special occasions such as weddings, baptisms and wakes.

"Make yerself at home and I'll put the kettle on."

Don't do that Bernadette or should I say Mary, there isn't time.

"Bernadette…"

"What…come through to the kitchen and talk." Conánn walked through to the kitchen.

"Listen Bernadette, or should I call you Mary…" There was a crash as she dropped the kettle full of water on the floor.

"Shit…what did yer call me…Mary...?" She looked straight at Conánn, "who the fuck are yer…my name's Bernadette."

"Listen calm down…"

"What d'yer mean calm down… I am fucking calm," she screamed at him. "Who t'e fuck are yer…tell me...tell me," she sobbed. "Ohhh no please don't…" she sobbed, "t'at was a long time ago."

"OK…OK…there now shhh, all I want to do is to help you. Now listen to me and I will help you. We can get you to a safe house, give you a fresh identity and you'll be safe. All I need is some information." Gradually her sobbing subsided and slowly the tears stopped. She dabbed her eyes with her handkerchief.

"How did yer find me?"

"OK…" Conánn codenamed *Poor-man* nodded, "with a little bit of research and a lot of hard work, some questions and some answers and hey presto I found you. But tell me, why did you suddenly run, my colleague was convinced you were dead?"

"I don't know…lost my nerve may be…who knows why we do these things, it was a long time ago."

"Well as long as you're safe that's the main thing, but why here right in the heart of PIRA territory?"

"Because I thought that it would never occur to them to look fer me right under their noses – especially as O'Rourke didn't know where I was."

"What were you to O'Rourke?"

"I thought yer already knew…I told t'at Sean…how is he by the way. He did a lot fer me yer know…looked after me…kept me safe and all t'at sort of t'ing."

Shit you don't know about Sean.

"Oh he's fine. He's on another job now so I'm afraid you'll have to put up with me." Jimmy gave her a half-hearted smile, which she readily accepted.

"Look, why don't we still have that cup of tea and you can tell me all about O'Rourke and your days at Uni." Mary thought about it for a few minutes before she agreed.

Later that evening Mary, or Bernadette as she was known, accompanied by her lodger codename *Poor-man* walked up Duke Street to the telephone box, she needed to phone her brother and her lodger needed to call his mother. Having made their respective telephone calls they returned home for a quiet night in. Within the hour a black Audi drew up outside 40 Duke Street and under the cover of darkness two people – a man and a woman – were spirited away into the night. Nobody had seen them leave and nobody was any the wiser until later the following day when Bernadette's employer called round at her house wondering why she had failed to turn in for work, only to find the door unlocked and the house empty. It was yet another unexplained disappearance of an innocent person.

Chapter 14

The secure radio in Richard's car crackled into life.

"Go ahead *Rich-man*. Over."

"I've had the checks run on Wyman and Seamus as you requested over…"

"And? Over…"

"Well, the checks I ran on Seamus proved nothing except for one thing over…"

"And that was *Rich-man*? Over"

"That he had connections with Rosie…over"

"What sort of connections *Rich-man*, was she his handler? Over"

"Ah his handler yes, but the connections were a little more than that… Seamus and Rosie were married…over"

"Married…I'm sorry *Rich-man* did you say married? Over"

"Yes *Beggarman* married. Granted it was in the early 60s…1963 to be precise whilst he was still in the Navy…"

"Sorry *Rich-man* to interrupt, but are you telling me that Rosie was his handler and his wife, over?"

That's interesting no wonder he reacted the way he did!

"Precisely…well not quite, you see the marriage only lasted a couple of years. Rosie and Seamus split up in 1965. I think the fact that Seamus was, at that time, in the SBS put undue strain on their relationship, he was away for long spells, and she was young and attractive – as you yourself know, so the inevitable happened, she met someone else, had an affair and the marriage foundered…over."

"I'm not sure that I understand, surely their domestic situation meant they were a weak link…a security risk over?"

"Not really, because at that time he was in the SBS and she was a civilian working at CSD Chessington, you know the place, the Civil Service Department. It's the department that

deals with the Civil Service and the MoD payroll... over."
Richard sat and thought for a moment or two.

If what you're telling me is true Sir James then how did Rosie become involved in the 'circus', who recruited her?

"In that case *Rich-man*," Richard asked depressing the send button, "exactly when did Rosie come on board, over?"

"Ah, I thought you might ask that, it was in 1967 that she joined the 'circus' initially in London – initially she worked for Five but shortly after joining them she transferred her allegiance to us over."

So I wonder who recruited her and did Wyman have anything to do with her?

"So who actually recruited Rosie, was Wyman involved at any stage? Over."

"There was nothing to indicate as such..."

Damn – so if Wyman is not involved then bang goes that possibility. I was sure he was a link.

"...so if there is nothing further, over"

"Just one more thing *Rich-man*, where are Wyman and Seamus now, over?"

"Wyman is here in London currently working on the Irish desk, but as to Seamus he is nothing really to do with our operation – he is with Ash and his operation so I would need to check through Government circles, and that could take a little time over."

But I was led to believe Wyman was in Libya, interesting.

"Roger *Rich-man*. You say Wyman's in London, over?"

"I say again. Wyman is on the Irish desk here in London, why? Over"

"Nothing really, it was just a comment which led me to believe that he was in Libya that's all. Incidentally are you talking Military Intelligence or Six where Wyman is concerned? Over"

"Wyman is Six but the Irish desk is a joint operation here in London. We gather information from Military and our own sources, we also receive information from GCHQ that may be relevant to Ireland such as possible arms shipments etcetera. This information is then disseminated to all interested parties such as Military Intelligence at Lisburn, Ulster and their Irish Desk in London, which is a mirror image of our set-up. Does that answer your question over?"

"It covers everything for now. I will be heading back home tomorrow as I am expecting a delivery at the company flat. I'll contact you again in a couple of days to let you know that I have received the package safely. *Beggarman* Over and Out."

"Roger *Rich-man*. Out."

Richard looked thoughtful, the protracted conversation he had just had with Sir James had certainly cleared up a number of points. Jimmy was clean and to all intents and purposes so was Seamus.

What was it about Wyman that still bothered him?

He pushed the thought to the back of his mind and once more he turned his attention to the attaché case on the seat beside him. The red dot – indicating the whereabouts of Jimmy's Audi – blinked as it moved further into the Bogside. Now it was slowly moving along Duke Street.

Is that where the girl lives?

The red dot came to a halt not too far from the Bogside Inn. Richard glanced at his watch it was nine thirty dead on when once more the red spot again started to move; only this time it headed back along Duke Street at a high speed. The operation was well and truly underway. Without giving his attaché case a second glance Richard eased the Mondeo forward and headed back out of the battle-weary confines of Londonderry and out onto the open country roads towards Belfast and the motorway to Dublin.

The shrill constant note of the alarm woke Fionnuala. Still half asleep she groped for the button to kill the noise that had impinged on her dream world. Having now silenced the strident noise that had brought her, with a jolt, out of a deep sleep she snuggled up closely to Richard's back as he lay alongside her. She gently kissed the back of his neck, and then nibbled his earlobe. She slowly moved to nibble at his neck. She then turned her attention to his back and gently kissed his shoulder blades moving down his back. He stirred and rolled over on top of her naked body, pinning her wrists down on the bed as he did so. She grinned up at him.

"Good morning Mr James."

He smiled back. Then with a sudden movement she was out of his grasp and had rolled from beneath him, turning him over onto his back. Then, before he had chance to move, she was astride him holding his wrists in a vice-like grip. She leaned forward and gave him a lingering kiss; her breasts gently rubbed against his naked chest and her long hair gently caressed his face. She could feel his body responding to her advances.

Mmm, how good it feels after all this time you're still as good as ever!

Suddenly, he broke free from her grasp and with a deft movement she was once more flat on her back, legs splayed apart beneath him. His hands fondled her breasts as his mouth eagerly sought out her mouth. His tongue pushed between her slightly parted lips as his rising passion hungrily devoured her. He could now feel her body responding as their basic animal instinct took hold and with one quick thrust he drove into her.

"Ahhh…I love you Richard James," she cried, "I love you."

Fionnuala, Fionnuala if only we had met…

He left that thought hanging and smouldering in his mind.

"Ohh, Ohh Fionnuala…"

"Ahh…" she cried.

Little rivulets of sweat ran down between their bodies as they lay entwined. They lay still, their passion like the pounding surf gently seeped away and once more they rested.

Bernadette awoke with a start.

Where am I?

Slowly the images from last night tumbled into her head, the fear she suddenly felt on hearing Conánn call her Mary. Her fear at being caught as they had walked to the telephone box in Duke Street, the way her heart pounded when he, Conánn, blindfolded her in the car. Yes it was all coming back to her; even the memories caused her heart to race.

I hope t' god these people are who they say they are, otherwise yer dead!

As fast as the negative thought popped into her head it was gone again.

They must be who they say they are 'cause why would they have brought me here to this nice house. Besides if they weren't who they said they were t'en why go t' all this trouble if t'ey were going to kill me. Aw come on Bernadette pull yerself together. Nobody is going to kill anybody and t'ats the truth now.

Her thoughts were interrupted as the bedroom door opened and Jean entered carrying a mug of tea.

"Good morning Bernadette. I thought you might appreciate a cup of tea." She placed the tea on a small table close to the bed then walked over to the fitted wardrobe from which she took out a white dressing gown. "Here," she passed the gown to Bernadette. "Breakfast is ready so you need to get up," she said rather curtly, still curious as to how Sean, her late husband, had got involved with this woman now languishing in her spare bed. "The bathroom is along the landing first door on the right. You'll find fresh towels on the side of the bath. You'll see a blue toilette bag with new soap, flannel, toothbrush and paste on the stool at the side of the bath, that's for you." Bernadette tried to ignore the brusqueness of her manner and asked the time. Jean glanced at her wristwatch.

"Five-thirty," she replied curtly.

"Five-t'irty yer say, my god 't is still the middle of the night."

"Yes five-thirty and you need to be ready to leave in one hour."

"An hour!" she answered incredulously.

"An hour; so there's no time to waste and we've a long day ahead of us." On that note Jean left Bernadette to get washed and dressed ready for breakfast."

Mary mother of God, an hour she said. How does she expect me to get up, bath and dress in an hour? That's without me breakfast –b'jesus this woman's unreal!

"OK Bernadette relax look straight at me now. Hold it…steady…steady." There was a series of clicks and flashes as the camera did its job. "OK…relax." The photographer turned to Jimmy, "well we should get a decent passport photograph out of that lot, but I'm not too sure about the wig though. What do you think?" Jimmy studied Bernadette for a couple of minutes.

"Hmm, may be you are right." He then shouted to Jean who was next door in the small dressing room. "Jean, come through a minute."

"What's wrong?" Jean asked as she appeared in the doorway.

"Need your opinion."

"On what?"

"The wig…do you think it looks right, or is there something else we could do?" Jean walked around Bernadette, looked at her from different angles, from far away and close-up. She scrutinised her through half-closed eyes and pondered on what she saw as the strains of Sinead O'Connor's love song 'Nothing Compares 2 U' played quietly in the background.

"Well, what do you think Jean?"

"I'm not sure. It definitely needs something." She then called a woman's name. "Jan...Jan. Where the hell is that make-up girl...JAN," she yelled at the top of her voice.

"Coming...coming. Sorry I was just in..."

"Never mind you're here now, this girl's wig it's lacking something. Remember we need to change her appearance as best we can. What can you suggest?" The make-up girl scrutinised Bernadette, stood back and looked at her from the side so she was in profile.

"How about..." she walked over and pulled the hair of the wig back, "if I had it back off her face?" Jean grimaced. The make-up girl shrugged her shoulders and let the hair drop back so it fell over Bernadette's shoulders once again.

"What about glasses?" Bernadette said in a quiet voice.

Glasses, yes now why didn't I think of that?

The make-up girl looked across at Jean. "What do you think?"

"Let's try them and see what happens."

"Give me a few minutes while I dig out a selection of frames," the make-up girl called over her shoulder as she disappeared into the next room.

"You do realize Bernadette, that if it gives us the right image it will mean that you'll have to get used to wearing them all the time." Bernadette thought about what Jean had just said and once more the strains of Sinead O'Connor percolated through the air as silence descended on the studio. Bernadette nodded.

"I'll manage provided I can see through them."

"That's not the issue – you'll be able to see through them all right as the lenses will be plain glass – the main thing is will the end result be what we are looking for?" Bernadette thought about it for a moment then shrugged her shoulders.

"It's OK. I'll get used to them," she said.

True to her word the make-up girl re-appeared with several different styles of spectacles in her hand and between the four of them, Bernadette, the make-up girl, Jean and the photographer they sorted out a couple of pairs that they felt would suit her facial features. Then with Jean's approval the photographer continued with the photo shoot.

"Right let's go for it. Come on Bernadette look towards me…hold it there…good…steady." More flashes and clicks and in a matter of minutes the session was completed.

"What do you think?" Jimmy asked the photographer's professional opinion.

"Much better," he replied, "the long hair frames the face nicely and the glasses give her an air of professionalism – yes definitely," he nodded approvingly. "It gives her the look of a career person. Now if you can give me about twenty minutes I'll rush these through D and P."

"What's D and P?" asked Jean.

"Sorry, it stands for developing and printing just a term we photographers use from time to time. Are you OK for time?"

"Yeah t'be sure we are."

"Good, then I'll get them done as soon as I possibly can."

Twenty minutes later and with the passport shots selected, the next part of the illusion had to be achieved. This meant that in the scheme of things Bernadette – as herself - had taken off on an impromptu holiday and needed some photographs to portray just that. It was decided that photographs of her lying sunbathing on the deck of a yacht with the backdrop of blue skies and blue sea would be ideal. By using this theme she could be almost anywhere in the world where it was sunny. She could be off the Balearic Islands, the Canaries, Greece or the South of France. Once the props and the backdrop of a clear blue sky were in place, the illusion of a bright sunny day was created by means of clever lighting effects, and the strong overhead lights in the studio only served to enhance the effect. The scene was set. The make-up artist then set about cleverly lightening Bernadette's hair and within an hour you would have been forgiven for thinking she had been away on holiday. Her bikini clad figure was a golden brown and her hair now appeared to be bleached by the sun as she lay reclining on the deck of a yacht. The camera shoot took a little less than thirty minutes to complete and the team had now created the ultimate fantasy, the complete deception. All that was now left for them to do was to make sure that the chimera they had produced would not only fool friends and family into thinking she was on holiday in some exotic paradise, but would also forestall any possible Provisional IRA reprisal.

Richard stood up on deck, the sea breeze tugged at his hair as he watched the Port of Dublin slowly recede into the distance. His thoughts once more drifted back to the cottage and his beautiful Fionnuala and their time spent together.

If only…if only…things could and would have been so different, but he was married and that was all there was to say.
He stood for a few more minutes and watched as Dublin became a distant blur, the ferry turned and headed out to sea. Away from the land the breeze no longer caressed and tugged at his hair, it now stung his eyes as it whipped the Irish Sea into foam and gusted across the deck, moaning through steel halyards as it did. He cast a final look towards the horizon and the faint outline of the Irish coast before it finally disappeared from view and with eyes watering he made his way back below decks and the welcoming warmth of the cafeteria. It was time for a coffee and time to plan his next move.

It was already dark as the Irish ferry berthed in Holyhead and Richard still had over three hundred miles to go so he would not be back in Kent until the early hours. It was time to put in a call to Paul and to find out what had been happening in his absence.

"Hi Paul, I've just got back and I'm still in Holyhead so I don't expect to be home until the early hours. Any news from your end?" Richard asked Paul.

"Nothing much…" Then as if it were an afterthought he told Richard about Johnny Rains. "There was one thing…"

"Yeah, well what?"

"Oh nothing really…Do you remember Rains?"

"Rains…Rains?" Richard repeated the name more to himself than to Paul.

"Yeah, Johnny Rains, you know the bloke who came to us about Imanos."

"Ah yes I remember, what about him?"

"Well he came to see me whilst you were away and he had some interesting things to tell me." Richard was puzzled by Paul's revelation.

"What things?" he asked.

"Very interesting things, but nothing that I should share with you over an open telephone line, Richard we need to talk urgently."

"OK, I'll see you tomorrow and you can fill me in on what's been going on and I'll tell you what I've found out."

Well some of it anyway!

Chapter 15

The black cab drew to a halt outside a flat in Cavil Street East London. A young lady with shoulder length hair wearing a pair of fashionable spectacles, and accompanied by an attentive male, alighted. The man, who looked ten years her senior, paid off the taxi and eagerly ushered the young woman towards the front door of the flat therefore giving the world the impression that he couldn't wait to get her inside.

Carefully sited above the front door was a miniature closed circuit television camera. This high resolution camera complete with wide angled lens was there as a security measure to record the comings and goings within the vicinity of the flat. It had been specially designed and sited in order to blend in with its surroundings so offering surveillance twenty-four hours a day, seven days a week. As the young lady waited for her escort to unlock the door, two passing youths could not resist making some suggestive remarks. One youth dug the other in the ribs and nodded in the couple's direction.

"Get him; look he can't keep his hands of her, dirty old sod."

"Yeah, dirty lucky bastard," he said to his friend, and immediately shouted to the man, "she's a bit of all right, ain't she mate?"

The young woman's escort ignored the comment thinking, *why don't you grow up sunshine and do something useful with your life.*

"Yeah, nice legs darling," the first lad called to the woman as she turned to see who owned the big mouth. He then couldn't resist another uncalled-for ribald comment, "Yeah I wouldn't mind a bit of that myself, how about you Chas?" he asked the second loud mouthed yob. She gave the two a feigned smile as she tried to make light of their comments but inside she felt far from smiling. *I wish you'd hurry up with t'at door and get us inside,* she thought to herself as the second of the yobs spoke.

"Yeah I sure would give her something to think about." Chas replied both loudly and crudely as they walked on down the street. Just then the front door swung open. *Jesus about time too,* she thought.

"Right Katie here we are, one self-contained flat for the use of."

Her escort led her along a short corridor, then up some stairs where a short corridor led to a second locked door. Discretely positioned above the door was a second small closed circuit television camera, which like the one on the front door, was connected to a highly sophisticated video recording system which not only presented a view to the occupants of the flat, but also encrypted the signal and passed it, via a telemetry link, to a control centre near to the flat and also Thames House, the Headquarters of MI5 situated on the banks of the River Thames in Milbank.

Once inside the flat her escort showed her around. There was a small kitchen, not particularly modern, but all the same serviceable. The kitchen had a range of inexpensive kitchen units fitted, nothing special but adequate for the purpose. The décor was not of her choice but there again beggars can't be choosers.

Back home, she thought to herself, *I have just had brand new kitchen units fitted and bought a brand new fridge, now just look at these. OK so they are serviceable, but b'jesus they're out of the 70s, and would yer look at t'at fridge. The one I got rid of was more modern than t'is one. Ah well, I suppose it'll have to do fer now.*

The sitting room wasn't exactly state of the art furniture but it was comfortable and like the kitchen it was adequate for what she needed. There was a three piece suite, a low sideboard, a small dining table and a glass topped coffee table.

The late Bernadette O'Hara or Katie Donovan, as her passport stated looked around the room and gave an inward sigh.

If only they hadn't found me. Ah well, it's no good m' crying over spilt milk.

According to her papers she was a secretary employed by Barclays Bank Ltd and working at the Barking Branch. She was currently waiting for a transfer to Barclays International Overseas, which was expected to take effect any day now.

Perhaps t'ings will be better once everyt'ings sorted out.

"Well Katie what do you think?" Her escort brought her back to the present.

"It'll be foin, just foin," she lied.

J'sus what a place. Would yer be looking at that terrible wallpaper now, whoever chose t'at must have had no taste whatsoever! Oh how I already miss my little house in t' Bogside.

She suddenly felt homesick and very much alone.

"Right, now over here is a 'Panic Button' should you ever need it," her escort was pointing to a button near the door, "and if you pull down this flap," he was indicating the drop down door on the low level sideboard, "you'll not only find drinks inside, you'll find…" She wasn't really listening to him as she walked over to the window and looked down at the street below. She was daydreaming as she watched the black cabs plying for trade, the red London buses and the occasional cyclist dicing with death as he weaved his way along Cavil Street below; *once more she was back in her beloved Ireland, in her little house in Bogside.* Her escort's voice droned on and on until it gradually faded and mixed in with the dull rumble of traffic from the street below. "So don't forget, if the doorbell rings check it out on the screen…"

"Oh, sorry…I was miles away…"

"I was just saying out in the kitchen and over here there is a small entry phone." He indicated to the handset mounted on the wall in close proximity to the sitting room door. "The entry phone has an integral screen so should you have any callers and be here on your own, which is highly unlikely of course, then you should always pick up the handset, press here," he indicated a button in the handle of the handset, "and check the screen whilst you talk to them. Always ask them to identify themselves and to show an ID card. Of course all our people have ID and will never question you asking for it should the need arise. One last thing, under no circumstances must you leave here without an escort, nor must you let anyone in. Is that understood?"

"OK, OK." She gave a sigh of resignation. "So when do I meet t'is man, what's his name, Paul or somet'ing like t'at?"

"Ah Paul, he'll meet you tomorrow...I suggest you try and get a good night's sleep as it will be a long day tomorrow as there's a lot to do..." Her escort was cut short by a buzz on the entry phone, the screen came to life and a clear image of two men from the London desk appeared on the screen. "Ah, here are your companions; they'll be here until the morning. Is there anything I can get you?" She thought for a moment or two before she replied.

"I can't think of anyt'ing fer the moment, but if I do I'll tell yer..."

The sitting room door opened and the two men whom she had just seen on the entry phone screen appeared. She jumped.

"Who the f...oh its yer two," she turned to her escort, "did yer let them in?" she asked.

"No th..."

"In t'at case," she cut him short, "how in God's name did they get in? I never heard a key in the lock."

"Ah, that's because we all have a swipe card."

"A swipe what?"

"I'm sorry I forgot to tell you. All our field personnel are issued with one, allow me to explain. A swipe card is a card that has a magnetic strip containing important information about the person carrying it, and is used in conjunction with a coded input to unlock the door, that way there is little danger of keys being lost so compromising the security."

"I see," she answered as if she was interested.

"Anyway Katie I have to go now so I'll leave you with my two colleagues."

It was late Saturday morning by the time Richard finally surfaced and made it round to Paul's house.

"Hello mate, so the wanderer returns. Come in," Paul said holding the door open. "Go through to the front room whilst I make a brew," Paul said making his way to the kitchen. "Tea or coffee?" Paul called to Richard who had settled down in one of the easy chairs in the front room.

"Coffee please," he replied.

"So what was Ireland like?" Paul's voice drifted to him through the open doorway.

"Oh you know…nothing's changed." Richard's thoughts went back over the last twenty-four hours, how he had intended to stay at the Tara then at the last minute returned to the cottage and his lovely Fionnuala.

Ah my Fionnuala how I miss you already!

The memories caused a stirring deep down inside him and he allowed himself the faintest of smiles as he thought about his time with Fionnuala. Paul entered the room with two mugs of steaming coffee and in a trice all thoughts of the last twenty-four hours were banished from his head.

"So tell me Paul, what have you found out?" *because, whatever it is you've found out may well shed some light on certain things over there!*

Richard listened intently as Paul recounted how, because of a bout of conscience, Johnny Rains visited him out of the blue to tell him about what had happened the night they met at the Eight Bells.

"You say he was kidnapped?"

"Well not exactly kidnapped – those were his words – I would have said more like grabbed by three 'would-be likely lads', who put the frighteners on him."

Richard contemplated the implications of what Paul had just said and then a thought occurred to him.

"Do you think they were the same three who paid you a visit?"

"I'm not sure, but it did cross my mind," Paul answered. There was a lull in the conversation as Richard and Paul both gave some thought to what had purportedly happened to Johnny Rains. It was Richard who spoke first.

"You say he was told to record your conversation and then to use a litter bin as a dead letter drop?"

"Yeah that's right, a litter bin on Northdown Road, why what's the significance?"

"I'm not too sure at the moment unless…"

"What?" Paul interrupted, but Richard ignored the question, his thoughts immediately turned to his arrival at Dublin and being tailed by Danny.

How did Danny know to expect me off that particular ferry, was he tipped off?

"Well Richard what…?" Once more Richard ignored Paul's question as he thought back over his trip to Ireland. *Could it be that these three shady individuals are something to do with Wyman, if so then that would make Wyman 'Thief'?*

"Sorry Paul, I was just thinking…when I was over in Ireland the first time…you know when Rosie was killed, Danny had followed me. Now Wyman is Danny's handler so somehow he must have known that I was on that Ferry…"

"Hang on Richard I'm way ahead of you on this one. Johnny Rains recorded everything I said at my meeting with him and it was then known that you were going over to Ireland…"

"So are these three blokes something to do with Wyman? If that's the case then he could well be *Thief*?"

"There's something else he said to me…" *What the hell was it?* Paul racked his brains, *something like 'We are important people…' No it wasn't that. 'We are security, or we work for the security services…' No not that, it was 'security of our country is paramount.'* Suddenly he remembered, "…That's what it was, they said to him 'do not go to the Police as this is official and is bigger than you think,' then went on to say something about the security of the country or whatever."

"Hmm that's interesting. In which case it may well have something to do with Wyman, but whatever the evidence I'm still not convinced he is *'Thief'*. I think it is higher than him, I don't know why, it's just a gut feeling. Maybe he is an unwitting pawn in all this."

"So what do you propose to do?" Paul asked

"Right at this moment in time I'm not too sure." Richard fell silent and again he went over and over the events, checking and double checking every last detail. It still came back to the same thing Wyman was *'Thief.'*

"There has to be something, this is too obvious."

"Would it be helpful if I got in touch with Rains again?" Paul asked.

"No… leave it for now," Richard said shaking his head, "I've got a feeling that…" he broke off in mid-sentence realising Paul knew nothing of the girl in London or the safe house. *Do I tell him about Mary White?* Richard thought to himself; *why not Richard, after all he is your best friend so trust him…*"OK…" He drew in a deep breath *well here goes…* "Whilst I was at Jean O'Donald's I found this in amongst

Sean's papers," he tossed his copy of the photograph of Bernadette or Mary White to Paul.

"Who's she?"

"That my friend, is a girl called Mary White – a very important girl. She had connections back in 1983 with Sean. In recent times she became known as Bernadette…"

"So what's her background and where does she fit into all this?"

"I believe that her background goes all the way back to when O'Rourke was at university in the sixties…"Paul gave a low whistle.

"So are you saying Sean was involved in some double dealing?"

"No nothing like that, but she may well provide us with a number of missing pieces."

"In that case are you off back to Ireland then?"

"No not at all, she's already over here…"

"Here!" Paul exclaimed incredulously, "where did you find her?"

"Jimmy and Jean traced her whilst I was over there and she's in a safe house up in London. In fact I'm going there tomorrow to meet her."

What's more I am going as Paul Jones sorry chum.

"Whilst I'm up there I want you to be extra vigilant. As I said I don't believe Wyman's the main culprit, I think it goes much higher than him…"

"Like who…Ash then?"

"Maybe." Richard shrugged his shoulders. "I don't know and that's the honest answer, perhaps I'll know more after I have met up with this girl, so leave Johnny Rains for now, but just keep your eyes and ears open."

Chapter 16

Richard stared at the photograph that he held in his hand, *hmm, I reckon you were quite something back then.* It was the first time he had really studied the young woman's face in such detail.

"So, tell me about the sixties," he said as he looked up from the photograph he was holding. Bernadette, or Katie as she was now known, smiled at her inquisitor.

"What about the sixties, where would yer be wanting me to start?" she asked.

"How about with Magee College and a young man by the name of O'Rourke," he replied.

"B'jesus I've told yer people a t'ousand toimes about how I met O'Rourke, Wyman and t' rest of the guys and it'll be no different fer telling it again." The tone of her voice reflected the exasperation she felt at having to repeat the whole story one more time.

B'jesus t'is is really boring and I'm beginning to get pissed off with t' whole lot o' yer, Mr bloody Jones or whatever yer call yerself.

She took a deep breath and started to recount the story of her torrid affair with a young undergraduate called O'Rourke. How she had first met the once shy young man studying for a degree in International Politics at Magee College only later to become his lover and his soulmate. How, for a time they were inseparable. She told him about the flat they had found and how they set up home together. A faint smile flitted across her face as she remembered him chasing her into the bedroom.

'Come on Bernadette give it back to me, I need to meet James.' With that I jammed his keys down the front of my jumper. 'Show me how much you need them,' I taunted and in seconds he had grabbed me and thrown me on the bed. There

was no stopping him now. In a matter of minutes he had my clothes off and I his. We rolled over and over. Ah it was good. She suddenly realised that she had been asked something and he was waiting for a reply.

"Sorry, what was it yer said?"

"I asked you for his name?" Richard repeated.

"Whose name?" she looked puzzled.

"The other young undergraduate of course. The one you said O'Rourke had become close friends with?" For a moment or two she remained puzzled then she realized what he meant.

"Yer mean the one who more or less caused us t' split up?"

"Yeah that's who I mean, so what was his name?"

"Ah his name Mr Jones…"

"Please call me Paul…"

"OK. Paul it is t'en. This man's name fer the moment escapes me, but I distinctly remember his first name was George and t'at he was studying at the University of Ulster. I know he did eventually drop out of the uni and as such m' man O'Rourke never heard from him again…well so he said."

Now what was his name…George Inman…no it was not so…Inos. No it was not t'at either. Come on now girl t'ink…it was Imos…or somet'ing like t'at…Imm…B'jesus t'ats it…it's Inamos…George Inamos.

"I've got it; his name was George Inamos, or something like t'at." She smiled triumphantly.

"Could it be Imanos?" Richard asked.

"To be sure, yer right Imanos. Yes Imanos not Inamos. I knew it was somet'ing like t'at."

"Are you sure O'Rourke never kept in contact with him?"

She thought about the question for a moment or two. "I'm sure as I can be, but t'en who can say fer certain. I'm not my brother's keeper – if yer get my meaning." They both fell silent. Richard studied the girl's face then stared up at a point on the ceiling.

Now that is what I would call interesting. George Imanos and O'Rourke knew each other at university, but where does Wyman fit in with all this?

"Did O'Rourke ever mention the name Wyman to you?" She thought about the name Wyman for a moment or two before shaking her head.

"No I don't t'ink so, I can't say I remember t'at name," she answered, but her eyes told Richard otherwise.

Now why are you lying? What do you know about Wyman that you don't want me to know?

She was talking again but Richard wasn't really listening to her prattling on until she mentioned the name Lamar. This last name certainly got his attention all right.

"Lamar you say..."

"Yes t'ats right Ryan Lamar, why do you know him then?" Richard didn't answer her but countered her question with one of his own.

"How did you meet Lamar?"

"I'm not too sure now, may be at a party or somet'ing like t'at."

Could this be the same Lamar that Paul and I know?

"Tell me about Lamar?"

"There's nothing to tell really, he was just someone I met at a party." Richard sat back in his chair, his eyes closed as he pondered on what she had just said.

Hmm, seems plausible but...

Just at that point his train of thought was interrupted as the sitting room door opened. Richard looked from the girl to the man framed in the doorway. Jimmy quickly crossed to where Richard was sitting and whispered something in his ear, to which Richard gave an imperceptible nod of his head and Jimmy immediately left the room pulling the door closed behind him. Richard returned his attention to the woman sitting in front of him.

So Lamar came from Louth and according to what Jimmy had just found out he was already known to RUC Special Branch as a bit of an activist and as an occasional dealer in recreational drugs. So was Lamar dealing drugs at this party or had O'Rourke been compromised?

"Tell me Katie, were you ever mixed up with drugs?" he asked.

"Drugs, why drugs? To be sure yer ask the strangest questions, now why would I be mixed up with drugs, I ask yer?"

"Not such a strange question really, after all we are talking about the sixties and university life…"

"To be sure, now do I look like I was ever into drugs?" she answered indignantly.

How dare you even consider such a thing yer may think I'm stupid but I'm not yer know.

Richard had to concede the fact that she was probably right, but there again he was no judge of character when it came to who did, and who did not, take drugs.

"What about your boyfriend?"

She paused momentarily, at first she was reluctant to say anything in case it should implicate her, but then decided that it was so long ago there would be no harm in telling him.

"Well it was whilst he was in his second year we were at a party in some big house. The Police must have had a tip-off t'at drugs were being passed around because suddenly pandemonium broke out. People were running everywhere…t' lights went off and the room was plunged into darkness. Uniformed Police came streaming in off t' street. Suddenly someone grabbed hold of my hand and yanked me up off t' floor and dragged me after t'em. Whilst t' Police poured in through t' front door O'Rourke and I were bundled out through a door into t' basement then out through t' basement into t' grounds of this big house. A car at t' back of t' house already had its engine running and we were driven off at high speed."

"Do you know who got you out?"

"Not at the time, but some time later I found out it was his friend Ryan Lamar and some of his mates."

"So are you saying Lamar was at the party?"

"He must have been, but I don't remember seeing him."

"OK Katie let's leave it there for a while. I need a break and I'm sure you could do with one. I'll arrange with one of my colleagues to get you something to eat and drink and we will talk again in about an hour."

Outside in Cavil Street, although the noise of the traffic was incessant, it was a welcome change from relative silence inside the 'safe house', besides Richard needed to take a walk and consider what he had gleaned from his conversation with the girl.

If the girl was to be believed then there was one thing that was for certain, and that was O'Rourke knew George Imanos and Lamar as far back as the sixties. Did that let Wyman off the hook, was O'Rourke 'Thief'? What other revelations would be forthcoming?

Katie sipped her hot sweet tea as she reflected on the questions and answers she had given to the man they called Paul Jones.

As far as she could remember she had told him everything, well almost everything, apart from a couple of minor things like for instance O'Rourke's taste for the high life and how at one of the many social gatherings he met two very influential people who would ultimately influence his future.

She smiled to herself as she thought back to the heady days of the sixties and the parties she had been to. There was one party in particular that she would never forget for personal reasons, for it was at this party she had lost her virginity. She had always maintained that she had seduced O'Rourke but in essence it was he who had seduced her. It was a warm balmy summer night and they had been invited to friends for a barbeque. The wine and drinks flowed, the music played and the summer house beckoned. It was there they collapsed giggling onto the floor. She hadn't known him that long, but the wine had dulled her inhibitions and in gay abandonment they kissed and fondled each other. Once more she was that young woman on the floor in the summer house.

She felt his hand caressing her neck. His mouth eagerly sought hers as his other hand pushed up under her clothes gently pushing her thighs apart. She felt his passion rising. His hardness against her, suddenly there was a sharp stab of pain and a further hurt. She wanted to cry out, but instead took an involuntary breath as he gave a final thrust. The pain slowly subsided as he entered her fully. She felt him thrusting deeply into her as the music played. He kissed her neck then moved his mouth to her erect nipples, then with a suddenness of crashing surf and one huge thrust he burst deep within her.

It was for this reason she remembered that party in particular. Later that evening they were introduced to a post-graduate student called James O'Shea. James O'Shea, a young man from a wealthy Catholic family whose parents owned farms in the twenty-six counties and in the province, was studying medicine and was in his final year. He had two brothers one was still at school whilst his elder brother Breandán was already a wealthy landowner somewhere near Drogheda. He was to have a profound effect on young O'Rourke during the passage of time. This was one of two minor oversights on her part that she had failed to tell Paul Jones about. The second aberration or oversight was her failure to remember or recognise the name Wyman.

Hmm, he was so good looking t'at young man, I couldn't believe it when he came and chatted to me. What a dishy bloke. He asked me out and I agreed to go out for a drink with him, but like all these t'ings one thing led to another and the next thing I know we are in his bed b'jesus I was hot for it t'at night – O'Rourke never did find out thank goodness or that would have been the end of it.

Richard sucked in a lung full of the heavily polluted London air as he once again went over the question and answer routine in his head. Not once had she mentioned James O'Shea and yet Richard knew that she must have known him; especially as the entry in Sean O'Donald's diary had shown that O'Rourke and James O'Shea were great friends during their time together at Magee College even to the point where O'Shea had bailed him out when he got into financial difficulties.

So why is she holding out? Good question Richard, does that mean she also lied when she said she didn't know Wyman. He needed some answers quickly and there was only one way to find them and that was to get Jimmy to call in some favours from the old team. Richard opened the front door and motioned to Jimmy to step outside into the street, where he felt he could talk openly. For the time being the least number of people who knew about this operation the better and that had to include members of Five even down to the operator upstairs in the flat.

"Listen Jimmy, when I get back inside, I want you to thoroughly check out our friends Wyman, Lamar and O'Rourke. I'm certain our target knows about Wyman, but she denies she ever met him or knows the name for that matter."

They walked up Cavil Street for a short distance comparing notes on what they had gleaned so far, which was really very little indeed. Richard was still no further forward than he had been back in Ireland and it was now with some sense of urgency that Jimmy returned to the Irish desk situated in an office on the other side of town.

Chapter 17

It was a cold damp night giving rise to low lying banks of fog that rolled in across the mud flats of Faversham creek. The ribs of wooden hulls, smashed and jagged, pierced through the low lying fog just like bony outstretched fingers reaching, grasping, upwards towards the incandescent moon above. The light from the moon cast an uncanny glow on the phantom boats that emerged momentarily from the fog only to be swallowed again in an instant giving an ethereal feel to the whole area. In fact the eerie scene could well have been straight from a Dracula movie.

In the distance a car's headlights bumped and bounced around as it headed down the track towards the Shipwright Arms, a lone building sat above the shoreline looking out over the creek. Paul had purposely chosen to meet Johnny Rains at this desolate and lonely pub as he felt that they were unlikely to be disturbed in such a remote place. Paul's car bounced about as he slowly picked his route along the cart track. He manoeuvred around the biggest potholes only to bump down into the lesser ruts and holes in the dirt track. Eventually he stopped the car just short of the front entrance to the Shipwright Arms and parked alongside another two vehicles.

The Shipwright Arms was an old timber framed building, an inn full of character with natural nooks and crannies created by the timber uprights and the low oak beams. This was further enhanced by fishing nets carefully positioned over some of the beams; the odd lobster pot tossed carelessly here and there and of course various other items of marine paraphernalia such as a ship's chronometer, navigation lights and brass plaques. Mounted on the walls were a number of sepia photographs of sailing barges which reinforced the connection with its maritime past and the creek. The roaring log fire in the large inglenook fireplace completed the ambience of the place and made visitors feel more than welcome. The landlord, a rotund gentleman with a Dickensian look about him, was just about right for such an establishment.

"Good evening gentlemen and what will it be?" the landlord of the pub asked Paul who looked questioningly at Johnny.

"A pint of bitter for me please."

"And for you sir?" The landlord peered over his rimless spectacles as he addressed his question to Paul.

"A pint of lager please."

"Will Stella suffice sir?"

"That's fine."

"Thank you gentlemen, that'll be four pounds sixty, please." Paul handed him a five pound note, waited for his forty pence change then indicated to a table out of earshot from the bar and the other customers.

"Cheers Paul." Johnny Rains raised his glass in acknowledging Paul's generosity in purchasing the beer and promptly took a mouthful of ale.

"Cheers Johnny.' Paul raised his glass, "first of the day." He took a long pull from the glass of Stella. "Ah that's good," he said as he put the glass down. "Now Johnny, I've brought you out here in the sticks so we can go over things again – like for instance the night of your kidnap. Have you given it any more thought, is there anything else you can remember, no matter how insignificant you may think it is tell me, anything at all."

Paul waited patiently, taking another mouthful of lager, giving Johnny time to think. Johnny sipped his beer thoughtfully as once more he went over the kidnap in his mind's eye recalling every single move. He would never forget the cold fear he felt, so much so that every last detail was as if it were yesterday, no he would never ever forget that night, so it was easy for him to recall each and every detail.

OK Johnny, all's clear except for that red Sierra that's just pulling out up the road but you've got plenty of time to get out.

He remembered thinking this as he set off from home on that fateful night to meet Paul at the Eight Bells. He pictured the car in his mind's eye as he pulled out from his road, he remembered seeing it as he glanced up into his rear view mirror, but there was nothing unusual in that.

Sure the car was still there as he travelled from Margate towards Birchington, the registration number, what was the number? Come on Johnny think.

"Did I ever give you that car's registration number?" Paul was suddenly very alert; he racked his brains, *registration number.* He thought back to the night Johnny came round to see him, *cup of tea – kidnap, three men. Bundled into car.* The snippets flashed through his mind's eye as if he was fast forwarding a video tape, but he didn't remember anything about a car registration. He went over it again.

Eight Bells, Johnny says he was kidnapped. He told me that he had been bundled into a car – did he say the registration? No registration.

"No Johnny you didn't, so did you get one?"

"Yeah, well I think so. It could be a long shot but I distinctly remember a red Ford Sierra following me along the Birchington Road. It had followed me all the way from home, the registration number was G517OKP." He grimaced and shrugged his shoulders, "It may or may not be the car they used…"

"Don't worry about that Johnny." Paul pulled out a small notebook from his pocket, "you say it was a red Sierra with registration G517OKP." Paul glanced in Johnny's direction and smiled reassuringly as he jotted the colour, make and registration number down on the first clean page in his notebook. He looked up from his notebook and again he asked him if there was anything further he could think of. "No matter how trivial it may seem to you Johnny, it may well be the breakthrough we need in order to track these arseholes down?"

Again he smiled, hoping that even if it did nothing else at least it would serve to reassure the man that he was on his side.

The 'bongs' for the ten o'clock news had just finished and Trevor McDonald was announcing the headlines when Richard received Paul's cryptic phone call.

"My place ten minutes."

That was all that was said, that was all that needed to be said. It wasn't a case of Paul being terse, it was purely a necessity. It went back to the time when Richard was in the 'circus' and became the focal point of their animosity. During this period of disaffection someone within the department decided to setup a phone tap on his home number and he found out. Ever since that day he had taken great care in what he and Paul discussed on an open phone line, once bitten twice shy so to speak.

A black Audi with an Ulster registration headed east along the A253 Harcourt Hill in Ramsgate towards Park Road. As the Audi entered the area known as Saint Lawrence the driver slowed down and started to mentally tick off each junction on his right as he passed them by. He needed South Eastern Road the sixth one off to his right. They were looking for a red Sierra with the registration number G517OKP as a potential target vehicle. This was the vehicle identified by a Mr Rains as possibly the one used by the men who grabbed him from outside the Eight Bells public house at Wingham Well.

"OK Jean this must be South Eastern Road," Jimmy said as he swung right into the sixth junction on his right. "Bingo there we are straight ahead, one red Sierra."

"All right Jimmy, slow down and I'll get some shots of it as we pass by."

The single lens reflex camera whirred as Jean held her finger on the shutter button rattling off a good ten to fifteen shots of the car and the front door of 29 South Eastern Road where it was parked.

"Right, I'll shoot off round the block and park in that space we passed back there."

In a matter of minutes Jimmy was reversing the Audi into a space about thirty metres from their target. Whilst he parked the car, Jean changed over the lens on the camera.

"Jimmy, you keep hold of the camera and I'll just have a quick look at our target car. I won't be two seconds."

With that she was out of the Audi and making her way across the street towards the red Sierra. Jean walked along South Eastern Road momentarily pausing to casually look up at the front door of twenty-nine. Having confirmed that no-one was taking any interest in her movements from the house she then turned her attention to the car. Again she checked to make sure nobody was around before she moved in close. Another quick check up and down the street for any inquisitive bodies but there was no-one about. From her pocket she pulled out a length of folded plastic strip, expertly fed this through the small gap between window and channel rubber and with a deft movement of her hand she had it looped around the inside door handle. One quick yank and the door opened. A quick look towards the Audi, a thumbs up and she was inside. Once inside the car she pulled the passenger door to and slid down low in the passenger seat. Her next move was to open the glove compartment.

Damn it, it's locked. Ah well a sharp twist of this should do the trick.

From her pocket she produced a small skeleton key and with one twist the lock clicked and the glove compartment was opened.

"Bingo."

Now what have we in here? Aha, naughty, naughty. I wonder if you are authorised.

In the glove compartment was a small Walther PPK. She gave it a cursory look over and then put it back. She quickly and expertly rifled through the papers which had served to cover the gun – there was nothing of real interest except for one thing, a piece of paper with the name George Imanos and an address of a hotel in Canterbury scribbled on it. She quickly stuffed the paper into her pocket. Jean then closed the glove compartment and used the skeleton key to relock it. Next she turned her attention to the side pockets in the doors, but a quick and expert search revealed little of interest. Now she reached under the seats, this was more productive. Here she found a piece of an old envelope, although the name and address on it was quite faded she could just about make it out. This like the paper she quickly stuffed into her pocket. The rest of her search revealed nothing.

Ah well better than a kick in the face!

Slowly she raised herself up the seat until she could get a view out of the window. Still the road was clear.

One last thing, anything taped under the dash and of course a tracking device!

She quickly ran her hands underneath, but it was clean. Her hand caught a metal cross bracket.

Just the thing.

There was a slight metallic click as she placed the magnetic base of the tracking device up against the cross bracket. One last check down the street, she lowered the sun-visor and positioned the courtesy mirror in such a way as to enable her to get a view up the street. All was clear, and with a deft all in one movement she pushed the visor back and opened the passenger door. She rolled out onto the pavement, kicked the door shut, checked that it was locked then dusted herself off and nonchalantly walked on down the street where she eventually crossed over and made her way back to Jimmy and the Audi.

The whole sequence of events had taken little more than a couple of minutes if that.

"Find anything?" Jimmy enquired.

"Couple of bits, but nothing much. Interesting though our friend has a pea-shooter in the glove compartment."

"Really..." Jimmy raised an eyebrow, "and what sort of pea-shooter would that be?"

"A Walther PPK..."

"Hmm interesting...do you reckon it's legit?"

"Doubt it...do you?"

Jimmy considered it for a moment or two then shook his head. "Nah, not for a moment." They both fell silent as they watched the target house. They didn't have long to wait before there were signs of life. The front door of twenty-nine opened and a man in jeans and a brown leather bomber jacket appeared in the doorway. Instantly Jean raised the camera and managed to get some really good focussed shots of him as he made his way to the red Sierra parked on the road in front of the house. He looked to be in his twenties with sharp features, about five foot ten to six feet in height and with fair to blonde wavy hair.

"At least we know where he lives that's a bonus."

"To be sure Jimmy. It's a bonus all right...incidentally I've fixed a tracker on the car."

"Good girl Jean, I do love it when a plan comes together. Here pass me the radio we had better put in a call to Sir James."

Richard thumbed through the glossy coloured prints that had been rushed to him by special courier that morning. On the table in front of him was the full name and address of the target, plus a piece of paper with the name George Imanos, Evinrude Hotel, Canterbury written on it. There was no doubt in Richard's mind that both Jean and Jimmy had captured on photograph one of the three men who had snatched Johnny

Rains at the Eight Bells the night he had met with Paul, add to this the piece of paper that Jean had retrieved from the red Sierra and there was no doubt about their connection with Imanos. Suddenly a thought occurred to him, *could they have been the men who went to Brian Gore's office, it seemed to be a possibility? He must remember to take the photographs and arrange to see Brian.* He thumbed through the set of prints once again, *perhaps now was the time to track down Wyman and to talk to him. Yes it was now time.*

Chapter 18

Hidden away in a tranquil mews off Belgravia yet only a stone's throw from the heart of busy Knightsbridge is the Nag's Head, a small pub steeped in history. The wooden frontage gives it the appearance of a Dickensian shop and with an unspoilt interior it is a world away from the creations of the modern corporate chains. The pub is as individual as the landlord who has owned it for the best part of twenty-five years. This charming little pub has changed little in the last three hundred years or so and is home to a plethora of genuine bric-a-brac from yesteryear which adds to its charm. There are two bars within the establishment and it was the small and cosy back bar downstairs where John Wyman had arranged to meet the operator codenamed '*Beggarman*'. The centrepiece of this small bar is the cast fire range that dates back to the 1820s surrounded by dark wooden panelling. He had selected this hostelry on purpose, not only for its atmosphere, but also because it was hidden away from the hubbub of Knightsbridge and off the beaten track. Here he was sure they could dine in peace away from eyes and ears and yet not too far from his base.

Wyman, a man of average height, now in his mid fifties with thinning hair, paid off the London cab driver at the entrance to Kinnerton Street and walked the short distance up the mews to the Nag's Head. What he liked about the place was the atmosphere, no pushing and shoving like you got in the other trendier establishments. There was no jukebox, piped music or fruit machines, just good old fashioned surroundings, good beer and food. As you passed through the front door you were immediately transported back three hundred years into a more leisurely period and the modern day trappings were left behind. Yes, John Wyman certainly liked this place.

He pushed open the door and made his way down the wooden staircase to the small bar where the smell of beer and freshly cooked food pervaded his nostrils. He purchased a pint of Adnams Best bitter and selected a small table at the other end of the room where he could keep an eye on the various comings and goings into the small bar.

Who was this operator codenamed Beggarman?

Wyman looked at his watch, it was just after one and *Beggarman* was already late, so where was he?

Richard glanced at his watch; the time was just after one. *Damn, I'm late* he thought to himself, *come on, come on.* He knew that it was no good getting agitated, the cab driver could only go as fast as traffic permitted along Knightsbridge and once again they drew to a halt. The journey had been painfully slow, but at last the traffic was moving again.

"You did say the Nag's Head didn't you mate?"

"Yes that's right, the Nag's Head," Richard answered through the glass partition that the cabbie had slid partly open.

"Well it's not far now gov, it's just up here on the left," said the cabbie. "Do you go there often?" he asked.

"No it's my first visit."

"Well you're in for a treat mate. Nice little boozer, good food, good beer and not expensive."

Well what more could a man ask?

"You use it then," Richard stated in a matter of fact way.

"Nah, not really. Been there a couple of times, but I live Catford way. Couldn't afford to live up here, gawd and bennet, the price of property up 'ere you'd need to be a bleedin'millionaire mate." He swung the cab into Kinnerton Street and pulled up outside the Nag's Head. "There you are gov four pound forty please," he said as he stopped the meter. Richard pulled out his wallet and handed him a five pound note.

"Thanks, keep the change," he said as he opened the back door and got out.

"Cheers gov have a nice day." Richard admired the wooden Dickensian frontage before opening the door and making his way down the wooden stairs. On hearing the footsteps of somebody coming down the wooden stairs into the bar Wyman looked up from the Times crossword he was doing, and immediately recognised Richard.

So you're Beggarman and I thought you had left the service.

"Richard old man, good to see you," he said as he stood up to greet *Beggarman*. "Let me get you a drink, what would you like?"

"Good to see you as well John. I'll have a lager please."

"Would you like something to eat? I can recommend the chilli con carne."

"Then chilli con carne it'll be." Then like a bolt from the blue it hit Richard.

Got it, the voice in the Woodman's of course it was, it was you. So who was the person with long hair was it Lamar?

Wyman made his way to the bar.

"Yes sir?"

"A pint of lager and two chilli con carne please."

"Thank you sir, I'll bring the food over to you." Wyman picked up the lager and walked back over to the table.

"Thanks for coming to meet me John; I know that you're a busy man so it's really appreciated." Richard gave a smile, but his eyes said something different, they were not smiling. "Well John, where shall I start?" Richard studied Wyman's face for a clue, but he sat there as impassive as ever. Not a flicker, not a flinch. *So Mr Wyman what do you really know?* Richard sat in silence waiting for Wyman to speak. *Come on Wyman say something,* but all Wyman did was give a slight smile, apart from that he sat there tight lipped. The silence that ensued was excruciating. Even though Richard desperately felt like saying something, he knew he had to wait. His training and years of practice were so ingrained he sat there as equally tight lipped as Wyman, waiting for his move. It was a battle of wills as to who would break the silence.

"Two chilli con carne," it was the barman who broke the spell. "Can I get you any sauces or are you all right gentlemen?"

"I'm all right thank you, what about you Richard?" Richard inwardly smiled *thank you John for that.*

"No I'm fine thanks." With that the barman left the two of them in peace to enjoy their food.

"Well what do you think, good or what?" asked Wyman.

"Hmm, not bad."

"Not bad, not bad," Wyman said in mock admonishment, "I'll tell you this for nothing. This is the best chilli con carne you can get in Knightsbridge, if not in the whole of London." Wyman smiled and immediately the atmosphere took on a lighter note. "Now what was it you wanted to see me about?" Richard took his time before replying, he still wasn't too sure how to play this. Wyman was a wily old bird and had been in this game a long time so he had to be one jump ahead if he was to gain anything at all from this meeting.

"John…" He paused thinking carefully. Wyman looked at him expectantly. "John, I don't know what you've heard, but I need your help…" He waited to see what sort of response he would get before venturing on. Wyman gave a slight nod of his head.

"OK, please go on."

"How much have you heard John?"

"Oh this and that, nothing to speak of really." He flashed a disarming smile, "I'd rather hear it from you. Incidentally you know that I work for Sir James don't you…of course you do. You see a little bird told me you were back in Ireland asking various questions about me." He gave another fleeting smile.

"So there you have it Richard," his tone of voice hardened. "Cards on the table…I know you've been nosing around and I know you think I am, shall we say, somehow connected with things in the past…things that have happened to you and others. But you could well be barking up the wrong tree. So come on Richard, let's be having it, what is it that you actually want from me?"

This sudden outburst from Wyman had taken Richard completely off his guard. *How the hell do you know that?* He thought back to his recent trip to Ireland mentally ticking off various pointers as he did. *Who have I seen and who have I spoken to?* Richard went through all the people he had encountered when he was in Ireland and likewise ticked them off as he went.

There was Danny, Jimmy, Rosie…wait a minute, Rosie, could it have been Rosie? No, not possible. Danny then…nope I told him if he breathed a word he could end up by being dead and I'm convinced he stayed quiet on this one, if not for his sake, then for his sisters. No definitely not Danny. That leaves Eamonn and Seamus. Hmm…of course! Seamus was handled by Wyman, Rosie and then Eamonn. Eamonn has also been connected to Wyman. OK so which one or is it both of them?

"Tell me about Eamonn John, what do you know about him?"

"I was his handler once… but again you know that, don't you?" Richard raised an eyebrow.

"Really? So it was he who told you that I was over there then."

"Are you asking or stating?"

"You tell me John, was it Eamonn?" Richard stared steadfastly into John Wyman's eyes watching for the merest flicker, but there was nothing, even when he answered the question his eyes never faltered.

"No it wasn't Eamonn."

Thank you John, then that only leaves one more person, it can't be Rosie because she's dead so it must be Seamus.

"Tell me about the time you handled Seamus then." Wyman briefly looked away then back at Richard. That was enough to reassure Richard that he was on the right track. "So you did handle Seamus then. So would I be right to assume that you are still in touch or is that too presumptuous of me?" Wyman just shrugged his shoulders. "Come on John you were the one who said 'cards on the table' and all that crap. So come on give me an honest and straightforward answer." Richard waited. Wyman gave a slight sigh.

"OK, for what it's worth Seamus told me, but it's not what you think…"

"So what do I think John?"

"That I am working for the other side…"

"I never said that."

"Not in so many words but…"

"Well until I do let's not even go there." *Deep down I know that.* "However now that you've mentioned it, it brings me to my next point. Why did Seamus act the way he did, why did he knock me out and tie me up?"

"At that time he had no way of knowing whose side you were on. All he knew was what he had been told officially…"

"And that was?"

"That you had been invalided out with a breakdown, but then there were rumours that this was a pack of lies and that in fact you had been stitched up by someone; someone who was much higher up the ladder. In the meantime he stumbled across certain facts that indicated that there was a mole deep inside the organisation, possibly in the department, he didn't know. But there was one thing, when he discovered you at the farm and realized that you had found out what he was up to he panicked. He was then torn between his safety and his gut feeling about you, and that's why he reacted the way he did. He felt vulnerable and under the circumstances he decided to immobilise you and not take any chances, after all he didn't want you spilling the beans. But if it's any comfort to you, he did contact me and I contacted Danny with instructions to contact his sister. I believe Fionnuala then contacted Eleanor and the rest, as you would say, is history."

"Actually Seamus arranged to meet Eamonn, but on the way he called in and told Eleanor that he had left a package over at the farm and she found me there. Well that's the way I understand it."

"Ah, he also told me. So being the cunning old devil he is he made sure you were found one way or another."

At last Richard had won; John Wyman began to recount the story about how Seamus had linked up with Sean, who told him of his suspicions about there being a mole within the organisation and how it was known in some circles that other operations had gone sour, about operators being lost and a hundred and one other things. In fact Wyman told him everything he knew including his personal connection with Lamar. How he had gone out of his way to befriend him and to gain his trust with the view of 'turning' him. Of course he had known for some time that Lamar was the enemy but that gave him all the more reason to befriend him. The Government desperately needed information and Lamar was Wyman's way in. In the end he had so inveigled himself into Lamar's confidence that the man was convinced that he was on their side and as such started to volunteer information. As the afternoon wore on the two of them hatched a plan, a plan that they hoped would trap the mole and at last *Rich-man, Poor-man, Beggarman and Thief* would be reunited for the final chapter thus drawing to a close the Ferryman saga.

.

Chapter 19

RAF Manston seemed bleak and uninviting at any time of the year, but a hangar at five in the morning on a cold winter's day was the last place to be if you enjoyed your home comforts. The wind outside whistled across the wide open runway blowing around flurries of snow, mixed in with minute ice particles as sharp as needles. With no protection offered, the wind showed no mercy, whipping the snow and ice up, causing it to swirl about like a mad dervish. Throwing snow and ice hard against your face, pricking and stabbing it like a thousand needles. The icy battering was relentless, causing the eyes to water. Yes Richard could certainly think of better places to be than RAF Manston to be at five in the morning.

"Right Mr James, just give us a few words so we can make sure that everything is working before you go to the hangar, after all there's no point in you being wired if we can't hear you. Just talk in a normal voice as if you were having a conversation with somebody, anybody, me for example."

"You mean like this, how are you feeling John, a little nervous may be?"

"That's fine, thank you. One last thing, Mr Wyman…"

"Yeah."

"It's important *Thief* thinks that Mr James believes you to be the 'mole' and you must act as if you are the enemy. If you are ordered, and I suspect you will be ordered to search Mr James, do it convincingly but be careful not to disturb the wire too much otherwise we could have a problem picking him up. Is there anything you need to know before you take up your positions?"

"Yes, what about Jimmy and Jean, are they here yet?"

"Yep, they're already in position. Any other questions?" The man from the communication section asked.

"I haven't, I presume you're clear on everything John?" Wyman nodded in agreement.

"Well gentlemen let's synchronize our watches, the time is now…" The communications man started to count down the seconds. "Five…four…three…two…one 05:15. Good luck gentlemen."

Richard glanced at his watch it was now 06:15 and still no sign of *Thief.* Everyone had been in position for an hour or in the case of Jimmy and Jean it was longer.

My God it's cold in this hangar. I hope I'm right about this and that I haven't cocked things up. He looked at his watch again 06:17 and still there was no sign of anyone. *Where are you Thief, am I totally wrong about this, have I misread the situation?* Richard was now having grave doubts about the operation, thinking that perhaps he was wrong after all. *I'll give it until 06:30 and if he Thief hasn't shown by then…* Just then his thoughts were interrupted by the strident ringing of a telephone in hangar. Then it stopped. He breathed an inward sigh of relief. That was the signal that a car was approaching. *At last Thief was on his way.* He glanced at his watch, 06:28. Again the strident ring of the telephone. *Good that means he has passed the Control Tower and will be in here within the next couple of minutes.* At 06:30 dead on the dot Richard heard the sound of footsteps but couldn't make out who it was. *Time to start the ball rolling.*

"So Wyman, tell me, why you?" Richard shouted across the deserted hangar. "Come on Wyman tell me…why you…" His shouts were met by a stony silence.

Come on Wyman answer me, I know you're there.
Richard walked further out into the centre of the hangar. He spun round in a circle looking for Wyman. "Come on Wyman…I know you're here…so cut the crap and tell me…why you…" Over to his left he heard a noise. He turned

sharply to face where the noise had emanated from. Holding his breath he listened carefully for any further tell-tale sounds, but nothing. Only a stony silence ensued. He could hear himself breathing heavily in expectation of something happening. He could feel the pounding of his heart deep inside his chest, it was pounding so hard he could almost hear it.

Shit Wyman where are you?

"I'll say it again…tell me why…" Richard's voice echoed around the hangar. Another noise over to his left this time. He spun round to face the place where he thought the sound came from.

"What do you mean why me?" A voice, that of Wyman's, echoed through the hangar out of the darkness.

"You know what I mean…so tell me why you Wyman, was it for money…"

"Damn you James…damn you…"

"Was it for power then?"

"I say again damn you James…damn your very soul. You should have died that night on Riley's farm; you must remember…it was the night Racain bought it…the night Jock caught a packet…"

"Yeah I know Wyman…it was the night…"

"The night the lights should have gone out but didn't…" His voice echoed eerily around the hangar.

"So what do we do now Wyman, what do we do now?" Richard shouted back into the shadows, but silence greeted his last comment. "Wyman…are you still there?"

"Yeah, I'm here James…"

"Well…"

"Well what?"

"Well what do we do now; I mean to say…you were the man in charge of the intelligence about the power lines…"

"So what?" Wyman snapped in a derisory way.

"Well if anyone should have known about the back-up generator you should…" This last comment was met with a chuckle of disdain as Wyman stepped out of the shadows. There was a glint of metallic grey as the light from the overhead hangar lights reflected off the barrel of Wyman's Browning.

Well that certainly answers that.

"Ah I see…" Richard sucked in a deep breath before going on "I think that answers my question."

"So Richard, at last you've got the message!" A second voice greeted him from somewhere deep in the shadows, a voice with an Irish accent that he instantly recognized as that of Major O'Rourke. He turned just in time to see the Major step forward out of the shadows. "You see," O'Rourke continued, "Wyman has set you up again." O'Rourke moved closer, he was now between Wyman and Richard. "Unfortunately Richard you seem to have got in his way and that was your downfall, because that meant a problem for me. After all Wyman was one of the best operators in the 'circus' and when things went tits up at Riley's place the department, or should I say Wyman, had to bail you out. Unfortunately we can't afford mistakes they are too costly and you Richard were the mistake." At this point O'Rourke allowed a fleeting smile to touch his lips.

So you think I'm the mistake do you Thief!

"Wyman," O'Rourke snapped, "tie him up, I've got him covered," he shouted as he whipped out a Walther PPK. Wyman replaced his weapon in his shoulder holster as he moved forward towards Richard. He grabbed hold of Richard's arms and roughly jerked them behind his back and expertly immobilised them with a plastic tie-wrap.

All right Wyman, not so rough…easy now.

"Search him Wyman," O'Rourke barked, "make sure he is unarmed." Wyman, a past master at searching people, ran his hands expertly over Richard's person searching for any trace of a weapon.

Be careful you don't pull out my wire Wyman because we'll be right in the shit if you do!

"Is he clean?"

Wyman nodded. "Yes Major."

So Richard James you thought you could outsmart me. There have been better men than you try, but you've got to get up really early to catch this Irishman!

"So at last Mr James we can now talk openly. Yes you were right, Wyman here was in charge of intelligence at Riley's farm, and he also got you out. Don't forget he was also working with Eamonn – remember him...yes Mr James Eamonn the Northern Area Commander of the OIRA and a great friend of O'Shea no less. All very convenient wasn't it. Any questions Mr James?"

Yes I've plenty of questions but they'll keep, that is except one that has bothered me for some years.

"Why was O'Donald killed?" O'Rourke looked puzzled by Richard's question.

"I'm not sure what you mean by that..."

"Exactly what I said, why was O'Donald killed?"

It's obvious that you have a problem with that question so I'll tell you the answer.

"Didn't you know, O'Donald was killed because he knew too much...I thought you of all people would have known...there is a mole in the department and O'Donald put in a report along those lines, or weren't you aware of that?"

"Oh yes I was aware of that all right..." O'Rourke smiled, "but as you know a mole has to be dealt with quickly and efficiently once he or she has been caught and we have caught the mole, haven't we Mr Wyman?" He turned to face Wyman, "So Wyman, tell our friend here why your intelligence about Riley's farm had overlooked the standby generator...why you wanted him removed." He paused to make sure that the implication of what he had just said had not been wasted, and allowed the faintest of smiles before going on. "Go on Wyman, tell him why you had O'Donald killed...or shall I?"

The disembodied echo of O'Rourke's voice and the words of his last statement gradually subsided and a heavy silence descended.

"Perhaps I could help." The silence was broken as another man's voice echoed across the hangar. O'Rourke, taken completely off guard by this interruption, spun round just in time to see Jimmy emerge from the shadows. In his hand he held a Browning levelled at a point in the centre of O'Rourke's forehead. O'Rourke raised his Walther in line with Jimmy's chest.

"Don't even think about it O'Rourke." A female voice fairly spat out the words that echoed across the hangar. O'Rourke spun round. There was a flash of gun metal grey as the light glinted on the Browning which protruded from the neatly manicured hand of Jean O'Donald. "I think it's time we all had a chat, don't you Major?" she said in a much softer tone, then in a voice that meant every word, "drop the gun...NOW!"

O'Rourke released his grip and the resulting clatter of his Walther hitting the concrete floor reverberated throughout the hangar. Wyman ran forward to retrieve the gun, too late he realised his error as O'Rourke's carefully aimed kick landed, crunch, right against his shin. There was a sickening 'crack' as the bone snapped and Wyman screamed in pain as he collapsed in a heap on the concrete floor. O'Rourke grabbed his opportunity and ran towards the hangar door.

"Go! Go! Go!" Richard's voice rang out.

Suddenly pandemonium ensued. The hangar was bathed in light. There was an imperceptible hum as the huge steel hangar doors that O'Rourke was desperate to make, started to close. From outside the shrill two tone sirens of a number of approaching Police vehicles could be heard. There was the clatter of boots on concrete as some thirty or more soldiers streamed in through the now rapidly closing hangar doors. Orders were being hurled at the armed personnel by their officers and still O'Rourke tried to make it to the doors, but to no avail.

With O'Rourke safely apprehended Jimmy severed the tie-wrap around Richard's wrists and Jean administered comfort to the unfortunate Wyman whilst they awaited the arrival of the ambulance.

"What made you suspect O'Rourke?" asked Wyman.

"It was something Jean had said a long time ago." Jean looked puzzled.

"What did I say?"

"You said that I must have upset somebody who was high up in the organisation and that got me thinking but the real test was when I started to retrace my past. The clues were there all the time..."

"Such as?" asked Wyman.

"There was the incident of Austen being arrested – I must admit that initially I did have you down as the prime suspect because you were his handler. Then there was the farm fiasco – again I had you in the frame because you were in charge of the intelligence."

"So why didn't you finger me?"

"I nearly did, especially when I found out that back in the 60s you became a great friend of O'Rourke and later recruited him. On the other hand I couldn't link you to Paul and my arrest, or with Paul being setup, so you see it couldn't have been you."

Wyman fell silent for a moment or two whilst he considered what Richard had said before he asked his next question.

"OK, so you eliminated me, but that doesn't explain how you came up with O'Rourke..."

"Oh that was the easy part," Richard glibly replied. "You see once you were out of the frame I got Jimmy to check out a few things and it soon became apparent that you and Eamonn had filed a full intelligence report about Riley's farm into Lisburn and it is protocol that a copy of all reports go to the London desk and who is in charge of London, none other than our friend Major O'Rourke. However that in itself was not totally conclusive as many eyes would see just such a report so I had to dig further, and with Jimmy and Jean's help we turned up an ex-girlfriend of O'Rourke's from his days at the University of Ulster – she told us a lot. For instance how he had become great friends with James O'Shea, who had bailed him out financially. Once I had linked him to the O'Shea family, just as you did back in the 60s, it wasn't long before I realized that he was a double, the only problem was he was tainted and very ruthless. He had eliminated many colleagues without the slightest suspicion. He even eliminated Sean O'Donald…"

Jean looked puzzled by this revelation. "How was he implicated in Sean's murder?" she asked.

"He was an Intelligence Officer…a double agent…he was also tainted and in charge of Intelligence for the Northern Command, initially OIRA but latterly PIRA. As a British Intelligence Officer he arranged that it be known in the right circles…the UDA…that Sean was a double agent turned by the IRA and the rest as they say is history."

"But I thought Ash said it was an IRA killing."

"That's true Jean, Ash firmly believed that it was an IRA killing because that piece of lowlife," Richard pointed in the general direction of O'Rourke, "announced at the briefing about the proposed attack on Riley's place, that it was Riley who had arranged Sean's death."

"The miserable piece of …bah, words are too good for that bastard."

"But why have you removed from circulation, why stop at that when he could have had you killed?" Jimmy asked.

"Well to have me killed would prove a little difficult because that would mean a Police investigation and besides I was not a major issue. Well not until my arrest ..."

"I don't understand. What was the purpose of trying to eliminate you after the 'slab' Riley affair?"

"He wasn't after me Jimmy; he was actually after Wyman..."

"Why me?" Wyman interrupted.

"Because my friend, being a wily old bird and a past master at this game he figured that it would only be a matter of time before you started asking some very embarrassing questions as to how Riley appeared to have advanced information about the attack on his place that night and as to how he knew far enough in advance to install additional standby generators. That sort of information could only have come from one source and that was a member of our team." Richard turned to O'Rourke, who had now been 'cuffed and escorted back to the small group of people surrounding the injured Wyman. "That's right isn't it O'Rourke?"

"Yeah that's right; you were always a clever bastard," he sneered. "I should have spotted the danger and taken you out when I had the chance!"

"But you didn't," Richard answered as he turned away to once more face his friends. It was then he noticed the puzzled look on Jean's face.

"What's wrong Jean?" he asked.

"It doesn't make sense..."

"What doesn't make sense?"

"Well, why were you more of a problem after your arrest than you were before?"

"Because an army lad called Jamie, who was the son of one of my men, had recognised the face of a well known activist from his tours in Belfast, over here in Canterbury. The man's name was Lamar, a fully paid up member of the Irish Republican Socialist Party, who was known to come from County Louth. Anyway according to Jamie the RUC's Special Branch had this Lamar character under surveillance as a suspected terrorist when he disappeared off the face of the earth, then about six months later he resurfaced in Canterbury…"

"But how does that fit in with you?"

"Well it turned out that Lamar was IRA and a great friend of Mr Imanos who was in my unit, of course at the time we were unaware of the connection. Anyway, as you and I now know Imanos was an active IRA contact, passing back information about us to his Chief of Intelligence who of course turned out to be O'Rourke. Once we were released without charge O'Rourke had to act. He convinced Colonel Ash that I was a weak link and the net was closed so I was effectively isolated from the department and in order to divert any possible suspicion, he then arranged my removal to a psychiatric unit where I was sectioned so that should anything ever come out, it would be the ravings of a mad man. Clever idea, but thanks to you Jean, Mr Wyman, Jimmy and of course Sir James I have managed to redress the balance. *Thief* has been captured and today is definitely the start of the rest of my life."

Also available from *Quill Publishing*

Operation Orpheus

by

Pat Monteath

Richard James returns to Ireland where he meets a man called Jimmy and very quickly they become good friends, or so it seems! Whilst in the Republic he again meets up with the lovely Fionnuala who certainly hasn't lost any of her Irish charm and he is surprised to learn that she has a brother called Danny who works for C3. There is a surprise encounter with the troubled Noel and a brief meeting with his old adversary Breandán O'Shea, but times have changed and things have moved on since his earlier visits to the Republic, but not for the better.

"There is certainly no shortage of exciting high-powered action, intrigue and suspense which, at times, borders on the disturbing and scary."

John Weller *Hull Daily Mail*

"The book is a well-researched and interesting addition to the military espionage thriller genre."

David Barnett *Telegraph & Argus*

"The mix is so complex and the confusion so total, no-one can trust an enemy or a friend."

Barbara Argument *Evening Gazette*

'Operation Orpheus' ISBN 0-9545914-3-7

Who Pays The

Ferryman?

Pat Monteath

As the Land Rover rounded the bend the driver spotted what appeared to be a wire at about six inches above the ground stretching across the road in front of him. Too late he realised what it was. He slammed on the brakes locking all four wheels; everything then went into slow motion. With all wheels locked up the vehicle slithered forward over the surface of the road. The driver saw the wire disappear from view. As the front wheels made contact and he sensed the wire go taught there was a blinding flash of light and an almighty BOOOM, then blackness. The force of the explosion picked up the Land Rover and tossed it in the air as if it were a toy. It landed a broken twisted wreck upside down some forty feet along the road. The blanket of silence that followed was almost deafening as the pitch black of the night closed in once again.

"He tells the truth behind the headlines in his trilogy of books"
Barbara Argument *Evening Gazette*

"Subject matter great, interesting story. Nothing irritated me about the story, in fact I loved it. The phrase I would use to sum up this book is 'Intriguing'".
Mark Druce *Ex-serviceman.*

'Who Pays The Ferryman?' ISBN 0-9545914-0-2